Suppose the Wolf Were an Octopus

K to 2

A Guide to Creative Questioning
for Primary-Grade Literature

by
Michael T. Bagley, Ph.D.
Joyce Paster Foley

Seventh Printing

Trillium Press
Monroe, New York

Trillium Press, Inc
PO Box 209
Monroe, NY 10950
(914) 783-2999

Phototypeset for highest quality by Trillium Services, Inc.

ISBN: 0-89824-087-5
Printed in the United States of America

Table of Contents

3. Children's Literature: Multi-Level Questions Level 2

Chapter 1

SPECIFIC PURPOSES OF THE BOOK

1. To demonstrate the procedure for building different levels of questions from children's literature.

2. To encourage teachers to develop questions from all instructional areas.

3. To encourage teachers to use multi-level questions in group discussions.

4. To demonstrate that higher level thinking can be attained through effective questioning.

5. To demonstrate that primary grade literature has the potential to arouse stimulating questions.

6. To provide a number of stories from primary literature, so that a range of subjects and topics are available to teachers.

7. To provide examples of questions at different cognitive levels.

8. To provide several strategies for questioning in the teaching/ learning process.

QUESTIONING IN THE INSTRUCTIONAL PROCESS

"In every age, in every society, there is always one who wonders, one who questions."

Eileen Lynch

Imagination can be enhanced only when one is given the opportunity to play with ideas, to discover relationships, and, most important, to ask questions. If, as educators, we demonstrate to the child that his/her ideas have value and his/her questions will be listened to, we are adding a rich source of fuel to that child's motivation for learning. It seems that involving students in higher level questioning will subsequently lead to a more open-minded, self-confident, inquiring person. It is our contention that teachers who actively engage in asking higher level questions will stimulate and increase the amount of child-initiated questions with teachers, family and peers.

Hypothesis No. 1

Teachers who show an appreciation for questioning, who establish a climate where diverse questions are valued, who consistently ask high quality questions will develop students who demonstrate greater involvement in the questioning process.

Students who are encouraged to ask questions are being given an opportunity to explore with their minds, to gain meaning for themselves and to relate new data with old concepts. The new questions, new theories and new ideas remain the most important part of the learning process.

Another benefit in using higher level questions is that it can provide an open-ended learning situation. When one seeks to ask questions about things or events that have no one right answer or a multitude of potentially right answers, an attitude develops where one appreciates the immensity and complexity of the real world data. Perhaps this point can be illustrated by the following quotation:

"Just when I knew all of life's answers, they changed all the questions."

Hallmark Card, Inc.

It is our belief that a classroom situation where questioning is held in high regard will result in an environment that is healthier, and one in which students are more receptive.

Hypothesis No. 2

Teachers who use higher level questions on a consistent basis will increase their students' higher level thinking skills in terms of frequency, depth, appropriateness and complexity.

This second hypothesis involves a concept which is paramount to our beliefs and practices. It is a relationship between good question asking and diverse thinking experiences. One of the basic goals in education is to provide opportunities which will stimulate the learners' higher level thinking skills. A method conducive to enhancing the students' thinking skills is an inquiry-based approach to learning.

QUESTIONING. . . THE BASIS OF INQUIRY

Inquiry is defined by J. Richard Suchman (1968) as a fundamental and natural process of learning by which an individual gathers information, raises and tests hypotheses, builds theories, and tests them empirically. If we relate questioning to this definition, several points can be made.

First, we feel that questioning is a natural process fueled by curiosity—a basic human characteristic. Second, in order to collect data, we must ask questions about the different sources, types and significance of that data. Third, when one begins to develop his/her own theories, we can assume that this person went through the process of question-asking; and, finally, one of the basic findings or conclusions usually generated from rigorous investigation is the development of new, unanswered questions.

If we believe that inquiry is a necessary condition for independence and autonomy of learning, then we must give serious attention to the role of questioning in the teaching/learning process.

We have taken Suchman's three concepts and related them to the questioning process.

Freedom

The more rules and restrictions thrown in the way of the child, the less chance he/she has for asking questions or responding to the questions of others. A part of freedom is autonomy and an autonomous learner will undoubtedly question.

Responsiveness

The child who questions must have a rich supply of data available when he or she wants it. Children who question freely and have access to a responsive statement are bound to come up with formulations that represent the way that child sees and attempts to account for the phenomena of his/her world.

Focus

Questioning is most productive when it has direction and purpose. It is the teacher's role to guide and assist the learner in focusing on relevant topics and issues, or as Suchman emphasizes, "discrepant events." These are events that present a phenomena that does not coincide with the child's knowledge and understanding of the world. A gap is created between what the child perceives and what he/she knows.

It is the teacher's responsibility to maintain the conditions of freedom, responsiveness and focus.

THE CLIMATE FOR QUESTIONING

In order for questioning to take place, the climate of the classroom must be conducive. This climate does not happen by accident, and creating it requires a conscious effort on the part of the teacher. A classroom that is full of excitement, a sense of wonder, and an openness to ideas, where there is thoughful consideration of data, a willingness to take risks, and a lack of concern over personal achievement—this is where questioning will take place. A classroom characterized by an authoritative text and an equally authoritarian teacher stifles questioning.

The teacher can shape the classroom climate. If he/she provides psychological space for students to ask divergent questions without fear of failure or embarrassment, the proper climate is likely to develop.

A climate that encourages students to think and question beyond the scope of the curriculum will yield greater student productivity and a more exciting learning environment. In recognizing the importance of establishing a climate which rewards divergent thinking, Torrance, P. (1963) suggests that teachers respond to students in the following ways: a) Treat unusual questions with respect; b) Treat unusual ideas with respect; b) Provide opportunities for self-initiated learning; d) Show children that their ideas have value; e) Provide periods of non-evaluative practice or learning.

Students who are exposed to this type of learning environment will gain confidence in themselves as autonomous learners. If the teacher is always didactic and restrictive or if he/she plays the role of the ultimate authority in the classroom, the students will develop a dependency on the teacher in an effort to play his/her game and receive the rewards offered.

Reason can answer questions, but imagination has to ask them!

Ralph W. Gerard

BLOOM'S TAXONOMY OF EDUCATIONAL OBJECTIVES

The basic framework for this text comes from the work of Benjamin Bloom (1956), who created the classification of educational objectives in a book called *Taxonomy of Educational Objectives*. In his book, Bloom presents six major cognitive operations: Knowledge, Comprehension, Application, Analysis, Synthesis, and Evaluation. In order to better understand these constructs, we have presented a brief description below of each classification.

Level	Description
L-1 Knowledge	These are questions that check the basic facts about people, places or things (information gathering).
L-2 Comprehension	These are questions that check your understanding and memory of facts (confirming).
L-3 Application	Application questions test your ability to use your knowledge in a problem-solving, practical manner (illuminating).
L-4 Analysis	These are questions in which we select, examine and break apart information into its smaller, separate parts (breaking down).
L-5 Synthesis	Synthesis questions are those in which you utulize the basic information in a new, original or unique way (creating).

L-6 Evaluation   These are questions which help us decide on the value of our information. They enable us to make judgements about the information (predicting).

According to Bloom (1956), the major purpose for constructing the taxonomy of educational objectives was to facilitate communication. It was conceived of as a method for improving the exchange of ideas and materials among test workers, as well as other people concerned with educational research and curriculum development. A more detailed description of the levels and skills can be found in Appendix 1.

Most educators will agree that the upper four levels of the taxonomy, Application, Analysis, Synthesis and Evaluation represent the so-called higher thinking processes. Questions that contain the elements or processes of these taxonomy levels are designed to engage the learner in behavior which requires a more abstract, sophisticated integration of content and experience. There is a complexity of thinking generated at these levels which is not found at the lower levels of the taxonomy, Knowledge and Comprehension. The higher level questions require the student, a) to concentrate and observe details; b) to relate past experience with new data for the purpose of creating unique relationships, and c) to judge the validity of this new information which might be used in predicting future events.

We have often heard that process is more important than fact (or product) and that, as teachers, we must consistently facilitate process learning in our classrooms, regardless of the proliferation of materials designed for the Knowledge and Comprehension thinking levels. To provide an equalizer for the preponderance of lower level curriculum experiences, one must carefully develop material, and arrange encounters for the learner that will stimulate and support higher level thinking processes.

In addition to using children's literature for good questioning, we suggest teachers consider using these practices in all areas of instruction. Good questioning can be used effectively in the following learning experiences:

Category	Description
1. Demonstrations	In demonstrating a new skill or learning activity, the teacher may ask students questions to facilitate meaning.
2. Discussions	General discussions about current event topics offer teachers an excellent opportunity to get students to think.
3. Multi-Media Presentations	Media can create a stimulating encounter for young children. The teacher can ask the students either general type questions or questions specifically related to an event or situation viewed by the class.
4. Field Trips	The effectiveness of a particular field trip relates to the ability of the teacher to raise certain questions. These questions will enable students to integrate previous meanings with the field trip experience.

5. Debates/Role Playing	These activities have great potential for involving students in questioning. They are self-directed, student initiated and highly motivating.
6. Independent Study	The teacher can monitor a student's progress in an independent study through questioning. This provides the student and teacher with an opportunity to analyze the knowledge gained and the direction the student is taking.

Questions are the creative acts of intelligence.

Frank Kingdon

While these activities are conducive for good questioning, not all questions are planned. A teacher who practices good questioning in all aspects of the curriculum will undoubtedly use questioning in a spontaneous natural way. Once the proper climate has been established, teachers and students will engage freely and openly in spontaneous questioning. This may lead to further inquiry by the students. It is our contention that thinking skills at a qualitative level can be enhanced through effective and appropriately-timed questions and discussion sessions.

According to Dorothy Sisk (1974), teachers need to become more aware that synthesizing, summarizing, and concluding can be done quite adequately by the students. Allowing students these opportunities will increase the likelihood that they will experience learning at a higher process level. If a teacher always has the concluding statement, the student realizes that this skill is one he/she need not develop.

How Can the Taxonomy of Questions Help Teachers?

Students frequently do not develop skills in using or creating ideas because they have insufficient opportunities to practice these forms of thought.

Morris M. Sanders

The following guide has been prepared by Sisk, D. (1974), for the purpose of helping teachers pose multi-level questions:

Question Guide

Purpose	Question
To build vocabulary	Do any of you know another meaning of the word "levity" as it was used to describe this situation?
To encourage interpretive thinking	Here we have further information and data; do you have any new ideas or hypotheses?
To encourage planning	How might we go about testing this idea?
To encourage predicting	What do you think will happen when Caliban sees Miranda?
To encourage creative thinking	How might we go about solving this predicament in another fashion?

The taxonomy of questions offers teachers several interesting possibilities relating to the teaching/learning. These possibilities will be presented in random order, considering individual differences have a significant influence on the usability and success of a particular approach to questioning. The following are strategies which integrate the taxonomy with various curricular components:

STRATEGY 1:   *Selection of Instructional Material*

> The taxonomy could be used as criteria for determining the appropriateness of specific content. Is the material aimed at a specific level of thinking and, if so, at what level and complexity?

STRATEGY 2:   *Building Curriculum*

> As one plans differentiated learning activities for students, it might be helpful to use the various skills, e.g., verbs, related to particular thinking levels. Kaplan, S. (1974) lists numerous verbs for curriculum development. Appendix 11, Clark, B. (1979) presents an interesting model called the Taxonomy Circle, which is a good technique. Included in the circle are the taxonomy levels, suggested activities, and possible products to be developed.

STRATEGY 3:   *Building Questions From Reading Material*

> In developing the questions in this text, we used both the taxonomy and verb delineations. It was helpful to have had several models and descriptions of the taxonomy while preparing the questions.

11

STRATEGY 4:   *Independent Study*

One of the major points in support of independent study is that higher level thinking skills are experienced by the learner in a natural, reality-based way. The teacher could analyze the student's activities using taxonomy as criterion.

STRATEGY 5:   *Student Selected Activities*

Providing students with decision-making opportunities is crucial to the educational process. We have seen one teacher use the taxonomy in the following manner: Students were asked to select from column one a theme, issue or problem. Next, they had to select a process from an extensive list of verbs associated with the taxonomy. Finally, they had to select a means for displaying their project, i.e., products. While this may seem highly structured, it does allow for student decision making, and it familiarizes the students with the process' terminology.

STRATEGY 6:   *Analyze Student Initiated Verbal*
                    Interactions

In group discussion activities, you may want to evaluate the quality and type of questions being initiated by certain students. Newton, F. (1970), has demonstrated that certain behaviors of an inquirer can be accurately observed and classified. Then we might consider using the taxonomy as a means of measuring student verbal interactions at different intervals during the school year.

The strategies listed above represent several possible uses for the taxonomy. We recognize that the use of these strategies will vary among different teaching styles. However, the taxonomy does provide some structure and organization to the curriculum process. If used appropriately (not in isolation) it can be advantageous to the teacher and student.

In exploring the uses of the Taxonomy of Objectives, Sanders, N. (1966), suggests three hypotheses:

1. Students who have more practice with intellectual skills will develop them to a greater degree than those who have less practice.

2. After a teacher studies the taxonomy, he/she is likely to offer students a greater variety of intellectual experiences than he/she did before.

3. A greater emphasis on the teaching of the intellectual skills (other than the memory level) will not decrease the amount of knowledge the student retains.

Three factors are presented by Sanders, N. (1966), which reflect the kind of thinking that is brought about in the minds of students by any questions: First, the nature of the questions. Second, one must be aware of the knowledge of the subject that each student brings to the classroom. The third factor that enters into the classification of a question concerns the instruction that precedes the asking of a question.

For the most part, teachers can anticipate the amount of knowledge students have on a subject and the mental process they will use to arrive at an answer.

The following points are offered by Carin, A., and Sund, R., (1978) concerning a questioning classroom environment:

1. The development of human talent and a positive self-concept hinges on the ability of the teacher to ask stimulating questions. This is basic to student-centered instruction.

2. The classification of questions assists instructors in determining how well they are teaching at the higher levels of instruction.

3. Proper questioning is a sophisticated art of teaching.

4. Higher level questions may be planned before class or spontaneously created through student interaction.

5. Fundamental to improving questioning techniques and formulating superior questions is the necessity of proper classification.

6. Research indicates that teachers specifically trained to ask better questions improve significantly in constructing and using them in the classroom. They become more adept at stimulating human potential.

7. Teachers who increase their wait-time in classroom discussions are likely to get more creative, productive thinking, longer and better responses, and a better quality of student-initiated questions. (Appendix III, *What Happens to Students When Longer Wait-Times Occur?*)

Teachers who maintain classroom environments in which students have freedom to ask questions, to theorize, and to respond to the questions raised by others will observe optimal changes in student behavior. These behavioral changes are described by the following student actions:

1. Asks a series of questions related to the one variable within the problem.

2. Sharpens a subsequent message to fine clarity after having had teacher seek clarity on previous occasions.

3. Asks to be allowed to get "his own answer."

4. Goes to data source spontaneously.

5. Follows the statement of a theory with a data probe to test it.

6. Shares a cause (theory) and doesn't ask the teacher to confirm it.

7. Shares an inference that coincides with data he/she has generated.

Some of these student actions may seem difficult to observe in any ordinary classroom. However, as one begins to concentrate on the effects of a questioning environment, one develops a proficiency at observing specific behaviors, such as the ones listed above. It is rewarding to observe these changes in student behavior, after having created an appropriate climate and practiced good questioning strategies.

THE ROLE OF THE TEACHER IN QUESTIONING

1. It is not the intention of the writers to present these stories in any particular sequence. All questions need not be used for each story. If desired, questions from certain taxonomy levels may be omitted.

2. The language presented in the questions may be refined or adjusted to meet the needs of the individual children.

3. We encourage teachers to develop their own questions for other stories they wish to read to the class.

4. Advanced students should be encouraged to develop questions using the taxonomy levels.

5. The questions may be presented to the entire class or to small groups.

6. We encourage teachers to practice longer wait-time when initiating questions.

7. In monitoring and evaluating the types and levels of questions, we recommend the use of a tape recorder. This procedure can be used periodically to analyze discussion periods where questioning is the focus of the learning encounter.

8. Listen to discussion periods in other classrooms. Compare your questioning techniques with the techniques of other staff members.

9. Discuss the different types and levels of questions with the students. Encourage them to use the appropriate terminology and/or classification system while they are involved in discussion groups or when they are inquiring about certain data.

Presented in the next two chapters are multi-level questions for fifty popular children's stories. Questions for thirty-five stories recommended for kindergarten and first grade students are in Chapter Two, heretofore referred to as Level One. In Chapter Three, questions for second grade students are outlined, representing Level Two. While we have tried to delineate the following fifty stories according to Level 1 and Level 2 Types, it should be noted that many of the stories are appropriate for students of other grade levels.

Chapter 2

THE FIVE CHINESE BROTHERS

Claire Huchet Bishop &
Kurt Wiese
Coward, McCann & Georghegan

Each of the Chinese brothers has a special talent or gift which he uses to save the lives of all the brothers.

LEVEL 1 (KNOWLEDGE)

* Match each brother to his own special ability.

* List the methods used in this story to punish criminals.

* What was the excuse each brother used so that he could send in the next brother?

LEVEL 2 (COMPREHENSION)

* Explain why the first Chinese brother was put in jail.

* Retell the story from the point of view of someone watching all the events.

* Show the events of the story in a mural. Make the events take place in the same order as they occurred in the story.

LEVEL 3 (APPLICATION)

* Prepare an interview with the judge.

* Relate what might have happened if you had been the first Chinese brother.

* Construct a model showing all the things you would find if you had been there when the first Chinese brother swallowed the sea.

LEVEL 4 (ANALYSIS)

* Was there ever a time when you didn't come back after being called? Compare your experience to that of the boy who went with the first brother.

* Identify events in the story which you believe to be true.

* Analyze the reasons why the first brother was arrested.

LEVEL 5 (SYNTHESIS)

* Suppose that the first brother could hold the sea in his mouth for a month. Create a new story telling all the adventures the boy would have.

* Create five more brothers, each with his own ability. Invent five more punishments that would not hurt them.

* Suppose that one hundred years from now there was a machine that could tell whether a person had really committed a crime. Describe that machine, and think of two people that might want to use it now.

LEVEL 6 (EVALUATION)

* Give the "Luckiest Man of the Year" award to the brother with the ability you would most like to have.

* Judge whether the first brother was guilty of murder. Explain.

* Do you think the first brother had a fair trial? Discuss how you might change the way he was treated after returning from the sea without the boy.

THE THREE BILLY GOATS GRUFF

Marsha Brown
Scholastic Book Service

In this familiar folk tale, the three billy goats outsmart the troll in a battle of wits.

LEVEL 1 (KNOWLEDGE)

* Where are the goats going?

* How were the goats different from each other?

* Who lived under the bridge?

LEVEL 2 (COMPREHENSION)

* Explain why the smallest goat went first.

* Explain why the goats asked the troll to wait for the biggest Billy Goat Gruff.

* Describe the troll.

LEVEL 3 (APPLICATION)

* Try to think of someone else who had a bad experience with an evil character.

* Choose someone you would send over the bridge to deal with the troll.

* Using the information from the story, paint a picture of a place near your house where billy goats could live.

LEVEL 4 (ANALYSIS)

* What other animals, besides goats, could have this happen to them?

* Identify some daily activities for billy goats.

* Analyze the thoughts that were in the troll's mind as he talked to the billy goats.

LEVEL 5 (SYNTHESIS)

* Decide how the story could have been different if the goats had all been the same size.

* Suppose the troll were a giant. How would the story have changed?

* Imagine that the Three Blind Mice were crossing the bridge. What might have happened?

LEVEL 6 (EVALUATION)

* Decide what you would do if you had to protect your smaller brothers, sisters, or friends from someone dangerous.

* Decide which character is most clever and why.

* Judge whether you felt the troll was tricked by the goats. If so, decide whether he deserved to be tricked.

STONE SOUP

Marcia Brown
Scribner, N.Y., 1947

A group of hungry soldiers stop in a town and ask the villagers for food. Not one of the villagers is willing to part with any of the food hidden in his home. The soldiers cleverly suggest that they prepare "Stone Soup." In the process of preparing it, the villagers contribute the same foods they were hoarding earlier.

LEVEL 1 (KNOWLEDGE)

* List the reasons why the soldiers stopped at the village.

* Give the recipe for "Stone Soup."

* Recall where each soldier spent the night.

LEVEL 2 (COMPREHENSION)

* Explain why the villagers hid their food.

* What was the conversation that the soldiers probably had amongst themselves once the villagers refused to feed them?

* Explain the role that the stones played in the preparation of the soup.

LEVEL 3 (APPLICATION)

* Cook your own "Stone Soup." Record your recipe.

* Relate what you might have done if you were one of the hungry soldiers.

* Select five foods that the soldiers could carry with them in case they become hungry again. Keep in mind that these foods cannot be any that spoil easily.

LEVEL 4 (ANALYSIS)

* Analyze the thoughts of the soldiers as they heard the villagers refuse them room and board.

* Compare the inventiveness of the soldiers with that of the villagers.

* Group the characters in the story into those who were generous and those who were not.

LEVEL 5 (SYNTHESIS)

* Imagine that the soldiers had not thought of making "Stone Soup." Create a new ending for the story.

* Invent a recipe for "Flower Stew." Write down your ingredients. Think of usual ways to prepare it.

* Suppose you were lost in the woods for a week. Prepare a cookbook to take with you, using only ingredients that you could find outdoors.

LEVEL 6 (EVALUATION)

* Judge whether the villagers were good citizens. Why or why not?

* Decide whether you would rather have one of the soldiers as your friend, or one of the villagers. Explain your choice.

* At the end of the story, the villagers thank the soldiers for what they had taught them. Determine whether the villagers really had understood what the soldiers taught them.

CINDERELLA

Marcia Brown and Charles Perrault
Scribner, N.Y., 1954.

This is the well-known story of a lovely girl, mistreated by stepsisters and her stepmother. Cinderella is rewarded for her goodness by having a fairy godmother send her to the Prince's ball. There, she meets a Prince who is to become her husband.

LEVEL 1 (KNOWLEDGE)

* How did Cinderella get her name?

* List Cinderella's chores.

* The fairy godmother warned Cinderella not to stay at the ball after midnight. What will happen if she does?

LEVEL 2 (COMPREHENSION)

* Explain how the Prince planned to find Cinderella.

* How did the stepsisters and stepmother treat Cinderella?

* Why did Cinderella's father never try to change the way his new wife treated Cinderella?

LEVEL 3 (APPLICATION)

* What three things would you like a fairy godmother to do for you?

* Select three questions you would like to ask each of these characters: Cinderella, the stepmother, and Cinderella's father.

* Design the gown you would wear if you were Cinderella.

LEVEL 4 (ANALYSIS)

* Compare the stepmother in this story to the stepmother in another story you know.

* Analyze Cinderella's thoughts as her stepsisters began to try on the glass slipper.

LEVEL 5 (SYNTHESIS)

* Many fairy tales make stepmothers into evil characters. Suppose the stepmother were a kind and loving person, and Cinderella was not. Create a new story and dramatize it.

* Predict some of the events that will take place after Cinderella and the Prince marry.

* Imagine that you are Cinderella. Retell the story showing how you would have treated your stepsisters and stepmother.

LEVEL 6 (EVALUATION)

* Select three qualities that a good mother should have. Evaluate Cinderella's stepmother based on these qualities.

* Choose the person in the story who you believe is the kindest. Explain.

* Decide which character in the story you would like to have live with you. Explain.

THE THREE WISHES

M. Jean Craig
Scholastic Book Services, N.Y., 1971

A woodcutter is surprised by a tree fairy. The fairy grants him three wishes in return for sparing her home. The three wishes are used up in an unfortunate manner.

LEVEL 1 (KNOWLEDGE)

* List the three wishes.

* Name the character who granted the three wishes.

* Where did the woodcutter work?

LEVEL 2 (COMPREHENSION)

* Explain why the woodcutter was poor.

* Why did the woodcutter wish for the sausage?

* Explain why the woodcutter's wife was angry about his wish.

LEVEL 3 (APPLICATION)

* If you had three wishes, what would you wish for?

* Think of things that you wish would happen when you get angry at someone.

* Tell how you would have acted if you were the woodcutter's wife.

LEVEL 4 (ANALYSIS)

* Analyze the woodcutter's thoughts as he went home after meeting the fairy.

* Choose an event in the story that you would like to have happen to you. Why did you choose it?

* Identify the events in the story that could happen and those that could not happen.

LEVEL 5 (SYNTHESIS)

* Create a new ending for the story. Assume that the woodcutter didn't care that his wife had a sausage on her nose.

* Invent several ways for the woodcutter's wife to cover the sausage so that they could still have their third wish.

* Retell the story. Have the woodcutter and his wife agree on three wishes that would bring them happiness.

LEVEL 6 (EVALUATION)

* Judge whether the woodcutter was a good husband. Explain.

* Evaluate the woodcutter's wishes.

* Evaluate the wife's behavior after the woodcutter told her of his experience with the tree fairy.

THE STORY OF BABAR
THE LITTLE ELEPHANT

Jean de Brunhoff
Random House, N.Y., 1933

Babar runs away from the jungle and goes to live with an elderly lady in Paris, where he quickly adapts to her way of life. Later, he returns to the jungle and becomes King of the Elephants.

LEVEL 1 (KNOWLEDGE)

* Where was Babar born?

* List the clothes Babar bought when he first went shopping.

* Describe a typical day for Babar after he moved in with the old lady.

LEVEL 2 (COMPREHENSION)

* Why did Babar go to the town?

* Explain why Babar stayed with the old lady.

* Why did the elephants choose Babar as their king?

LEVEL 3 (APPLICATION)

* Put together a list of jungle animals that are hunted.

* Use information from the story to make a timeline showing the events in Babar's life.

* Babar shared many activities with the old lady. Choose some of your daily activities that you might want to share with Babar.

27

LEVEL 4 (ANALYSIS)

* Compare and contrast Babar's life in the jungle as a baby with his new life as King of the Elephants.

* Analyze Babar's feelings and thoughts as he ran from the hunter.

* Compare your ideas about hunting animals for food with those about hunting animals for sport or fun.

LEVEL 5 (SYNTHESIS)

* Babar and Celeste left on their honeymoon looking for more adventures. Create a new ending for the story. Describe two exciting adventures they might have.

* Invent a way that animals could be protected from hunters. Draw a picture showing what you invented.

* Suppose that Babar didn't meet the old lady. Tell a new story about his adventures in the town.

LEVEL 6 (EVALUATION)

* Judge whether the hunter had the right to kill Babar's mother. Explain your answer.

* Evaluate Babar as King of the Elephants. Would he be a good king? Why or why not?

* Decide whether Babar made the right decision when he left the old lady and went back to the jungle. Explain your answer.

HELGA'S DOWRY:
A TROLL LOVE STORY

Tomie de Paola
Harcourt, Brace & Jovanovich
1977

Helga asserts her independence and power to make decisions about her own life as she works to earn money for her dowry. The person she marries at the end is not the one she originally planned to marry.

LEVEL 1 (KNOWLEDGE)

* Tell what would happen to Helga if she never married.

* Where did Helga go to earn her dowry?

* What were the three items Helga wanted for her dowry?

LEVEL 2 (COMPREHENSION)

* Who watched Helga's activities?

* Explain why Lars agreed to marry Inge.

* Why did Helga decide not to marry Lars, after all?

LEVEL 3 (APPLICATION)

* Choose the troll you would have married if you were Lars. Give reasons.

* Would you rather be married to a rich, ugly person or a poor, but beautiful person? Select your choice and tell why.

* Tell the story from the point of view of the troll king.

LEVEL 4 (ANALYSIS)

* Identify the parts of the story that could happen to a real person.

* Identify the parts of the story showing that trolls are different from people.

* Compare the trolls in this story to the troll in the story of *The Three Billy Goats Gruff*.

LEVEL 5 (SYNTHESIS)

* Imagine that Helga did not complete her tasks and could not acquire a dowry. Tell what might happen.

* Imagine some of the places or things Helga might have seen if she were doomed to wander the earth forever.

* Suppose that Lars waited for Helga and did not agree to marry Inge. Predict what might happen.

LEVEL 6 (EVALUATION)

* Evaluate Lars' choice of a wife. Explain whether you think he made a good or a poor decision.

* Decide whether Helga used honest methods to get her dowry. Give reasons for your decision.

* Award the "Troll of the Year" prize to the troll who you feel was the most deserving. Explain your choice.

LITTLE RED RIDING HOOD

Beatrice Schenk de Regnier
Atheneum, N.Y., 1972

Beatrice Schenk de Regnier's story of Little Red Riding Hood is the tale of a little girl who meets a wolf on the way to her grandmother's house. The wolf thinks he has found an easy way to give himself an extra large dinner. Instead, he is outsmarted by Little Red Riding Hood.

LEVEL 1 (KNOWLEDGE)

* Who saved Little Red Riding Hood and her grandmother?

* Why did Little Red Riding Hood go to visit her grandmother?

* Name the animal Little Red Riding Hood met on the way to her grandmother's house.

LEVEL 2 (COMPREHENSION)

* Explain the wolf's plans as he headed towards grandmother's house.

* Why did Little Red Riding Hood's mother worry about a trip through the woods?

* How did Little Red Riding Hood know that the wolf was not really her grandmother?

LEVEL 3 (APPLICATION)

* Try to imagine what you would do if you were to meet a wolf on the way to your grandmother's house.

* What would you bring to your grandmother if she were sick?

* Interview the wolf and ask him five questions that will help you get to know him better.

LEVEL 4 (ANALYSIS)

* Compare the wolf in this story to the wolf in *The Three Little Pigs*. How are they alike? How are they different?

* Analyze the wolf's thoughts as he waited for Little Red Riding Hood.

* In what ways could the wolf have resembled the grandmother? How was he different?

LEVEL 5 (SYNTHESIS)

* Suppose that Little Red Riding Hood met a rabbit instead of a wolf. Make up a new story telling what might happen.

* Think of other ways that Little Red Riding Hood could have been saved.

* Predict what might happen the next time Little Red Riding Hood goes to her grandmother's house.

LEVEL 6 (EVALUATION)

* What character would you like to be? Why?

* Evaluate the wolf's plans for making a meal out of Grandmother and Little Red Riding Hood. What mistakes did he make?

* Select the character that you think is most clever. Give reasons.

PIGWIG

John Dyke
Methuen, Inc.

Although he tries everything in his power, Pigwig cannot win the heart of Matilda. Finally, she sees what an outstanding pig he is when he heroically catches a thief.

LEVEL 1 (KNOWLEDGE)

* List all the animals who live on Mr. Brown's farm.

* Describe Pigwig's hats.

* Retell the story of the robbery, in your own words.

LEVEL 2 (COMPREHENSION)

* Why didn't Matilda want to marry Pigwig?

* Explain why Pigwig continued to look for new hats.

* Give three reasons why Matilda finally agreed to marry Pigwig.

LEVEL 3 (APPLICATION)

* Tell the story from Matilda's point of view.

* If Pigwig were trying to impress you, what would he have to do?

* Look for hats that Pigwig could have used, or create them yourself! Make a display of "Pigwig's Hats." Have a contest to see who can come up with the most original hat.

33

LEVEL 4 (ANALYSIS)

* Compare the way Pigwig tried to win Matilda to the way Helga tried to win Lars. (See the story, *Helga's Dowry*.)

* Analyze Pigwig's feelings each time Matilda turned him down.

* Compare Pigwig to Matilda. How are they alike and/or different?

LEVEL 5 (SYNTHESIS)

* What if Pigwig had not caught the robber? Write a new ending for the story.

* Suppose Pigwig were an elephant! Retell the story.

* Pretend that this story takes place on a planet in outer space one thousand years from now. Create a new story about this.

LEVEL 6 (EVALUATION)

* Judge whether Pigwig really loved Matilda. Why or why not?

* Give a prize to Pigwig for "the most creative hat of all." Which one would it be?

* Decide whether Matilda will be a good wife for Pigwig. Explain your answer.

SIX FOOLISH FISHERMEN

Benjamin Elkin
Childrens, 1957

Based on an eighteenth century folk-tale, this story describes how six brothers fear one of their numbers is lost, because each, counting in turn, forgets to count himself! A young boy finally relieves their bewilderment by pointing out their mistake.

LEVEL 1 (KNOWLEDGE)

* Tell where the brothers decided to go.

* Dramatize the events in the story.

* Explain how the little boy helped the brothers solve their problem.

LEVEL 2 (COMPREHENSION)

* Explain why each brother became so upset.

* Dramatize the events in the story.

* Explain how the little boy helped the brothers solve their problem.

LEVEL 3 (APPLICATION)

* How would you have helped the fisherman find the "missing brother?"

* Think of a time when a brother, sister or friend was lost. What did you do?

* Choose something you would give as a reward to someone who helped to find your brother or sister.

LEVEL 4 (ANALYSIS)

* What event in the story points out the foolishness of the fishermen?

* Identify an event in the story that has happened to you.

* Identify an event that you believe would never happen to you.

LEVEL 5 (SYNTHESIS)

* Create a new ending for the story. Imagine that the little boy was not available to solve the fishermen's problem.

* Think of ways that the fishermen could have counted each other correctly.

* Dramatize the story pretending that the title is "Six Foolish Hunters."

LEVEL 6 (EVALUATION)

* Judge who was the most clever character in the story.

* Evaluate the boy's personality traits displayed in the story. Tell whether he is someone you would like for a friend.

* Decide whether the boy was rewarded fairly for what he had done.

GOLDILOCKS AND THE THREE BEARS

Margaret Farguhar
Grosset & Dunlap, N.Y., 1958.

Goldilocks wanders into the house of the Three Bears, tastes their porridge and tries out their chairs and beds. When the bears return, Goldilocks runs away.

LEVEL 1 (KNOWLEDGE)

* List the characters in the story.

* What were the bears eating?

* Where was Goldilocks when the bears found her?

LEVEL 2 (COMPREHENSION)

* Retell the events in the story in your own words.

* Why was Goldilocks afraid of the bears?

* Why was Goldilocks sleeping in Baby Bear's bed?

LEVEL 3 (APPLICATION)

* Tell what might have happened if you had been Goldilocks.

* Relate the story from the point of view of Baby Bear.

* Use the information from the story to help you build a model of the bears' house.

LEVEL 4 (ANALYSIS)

* Compare Goldilocks' experience with that of Little Red Riding Hood.

* Make a list of all the events in the story that indicate it is a fairy tale.

LEVEL 5 (SYNTHESIS)

* Combine art and drama to create a new ending for the story.

* Suppose that Goldilocks had found the home of the Three Raccoons. What might have happened?

* What if Goldilocks had brought a friend to the home of the Three Bears? Imagine what would have happened.

LEVEL 6 (EVALUATION)

* Judge whether Goldilocks made a good decision by running away from the bears. Explain.

* Evaluate Goldilocks' behavior as a guest in the bears home.

* Pretend that Goldilocks was on trial for "breaking and entering." Decide whether you would find her guilty. Justify your decision.

THE THREE LITTLE PIGS

Paul Galdone
The Seabury Press, N.Y., 1970

In Paul Galdone's version of this familiar children's story, the three little pigs are sent away from home to gain independence. The third little pig is finally left alone to outwit and triumph over the wolf.

LEVEL 1 (KNOWLEDGE)

* List the materials used by the pigs for building their homes.

* Name the pigs' enemy.

* Tell which house was the strongest.

LEVEL 2 (COMPREHENSION)

* Explain why the third little pig's house withstood the wolf's attack.

* Why did the mother pig send the three little pigs away from home?

* Explain how the third little pig outwitted the wolf.

LEVEL 3 (APPLICATION)

* What building materials might the pigs find around your house?

* Construct model houses from the same materials used by the pigs.

* Think of some effective way for the wolf to get into the house of the third little pig.

LEVEL 4 (ANALYSIS)

* Analyze the third little pig's thoughts when the wolf came to his house.

* Examine the poor features of the first two houses.

* What thoughts do you suppose the wolf had as he attempted to get into each house?

LEVEL 5 (SYNTHESIS)

* Create a new story pretending that the three little pigs were trying to protect themselves from a man instead of a wolf.

* When the pigs left home, each one went off on his own. Think about other ways they could have lived after leaving their mother.

* Suppose there were "Six Little Pigs." Think of other materials that could be used to build their houses.

LEVEL 6 (EVALUATION)

* Tell which character you would rather be: the wolf or a pig. Why?

* Choose one pig to be your friend. Who would you choose? Why?

JACK & THE BEANSTALK

Jack exchanges his cow for some magic beans, and a world of adventure opens up for him. Follow his experiences in the Giant's castle and discover how he conquers the Giant and brings wealth to his family.

LEVEL 1 (KNOWLEDGE)

* Tell what Jack took out of the Giant's castle.

* Repeat the famous words said by the giant.

* Tell how the giant knew there was a boy in his castle.

LEVEL 2 (COMPREHENSION)

* Explain why Jack sold the cow.

* Identify three reasons why Jack was afraid of the Giant.

* Explain why Jack was willing to trade the cow for the beans.

LEVEL 3 (APPLICATION)

* Try to imagine what you would have done in the Giant's castle.

* Choose something Jack could have taken from your house that would have been useful to his mother or to him.

* Use the information from the story to build a diorama, showing the castle, the beanstalk, and Jack's house.

LEVEL 4 (ANALYSIS)

* What parts of the story could not have happened?

* Identify parts of the story that indicate Jack's family is poor.

* Compare Jack's dealings with the Giant to the way the "Three Billy Goats Gruff" handled the troll.

LEVEL 5 (SYNTHESIS)

* Change the story by having Jack take different things from the Giant.

* Retell the story, making the Giant into a kind character.

* Suppose Jack were a girl. Create a new story.

LEVEL 6 (EVALUATION)

* List three ways in which Jack was a "bad" son. List three ways in which he was a "good" son.

* Name the character in this story that you would most like to be. Why?

* Choose the character that you feel is most important to the story. Why?

42

HENNY PENNY

Galdone
The Seabury Press. N.Y., 1968.

Henny Penny sets out to take the message that "the sky is falling" to the king. Along the way, she meets her friends: Turkey Lurkey, Cocky Locky, Ducky Lucky, and Goosey Loosey. She also meets Foxy Loxy, who outsmarts everyone. Henny Penny and her friends never get to the king, but Foxy Loxy has a good dinner!

LEVEL 1 (KNOWLEDGE)

* State the reason why Henny Penny thought that the sky was falling.

* Name the person she wanted to tell this to.

* List the friends who were accompanying her.

LEVEL 2 (COMPREHENSION)

* Why did Henny Penny think the King should know about this?

* Why did Henny Penny's friends agree to go with her to the king?

* Did Foxy Loxy really know a shortcut to the palace?

LEVEL 3 (APPLICATION)

* What friends would you share your problems with?

* Tell what you would have done with Henny Penny and her friends if you were a fox.

* Interview Foxy Loxy at the end of the day.

LEVEL 4 (ANALYSIS)

* Compare the fox in this story with some other story animal known for trickery.

* Analyze the reasoning that took place in the fox's mind as he joined Henny Penny's group.

* What parts of the story could have really happened?

LEVEL 5 (SYNTHESIS)

* Create a new ending for the story. Pretend that the animals didn't meet Foxy Loxy.

* Retell the story with imaginary animals. Invent names for your animals.

* Change the story so that the animals meet an elephant instead of a fox.

LEVEL 6 (EVALUATION)

* Judge which animal was the most clever.

* Tell which animal you would have been.

* Evaluate Foxy Loxy's actions.

RUMPLESTILTSKIN

A. Garland
Doubleday & Co., N.Y., 1964

The miller has led the king to believe that his daughter is able to spin straw into gold. When the king commands her to do so, she is beside herself with fear. Then a little man helps her. Each time he assists her, she gives him a gift. The last time, he asks for her child after she marries the king. Only if she can discover the secret of his name will he not take the child forever.

LEVEL 1 (KNOWLEDGE)

* Tell why the miller's daughter was brought before the king.

* List the gifts the girl promised Rumplestiltskin if he would spin the straw into gold.

LEVEL 2 (COMPREHENSION)

* Explain why the king asked the girl to spin the straw into gold three times.

* Why did Rumplestiltskin come back to see the girl after she became queen?

* Tell why Rumplestiltskin asked the girl to guess his name.

LEVEL 3 (APPLICATION)

* If you were Rumplestiltskin, what gifts would you have demanded in return for spinning straw into gold.

* Try to think of a job that you have at home that you might ask Rumplestiltskin to do, using his magical powers.

45

* Tell the story from Rumplestiltskin's point of view.

LEVEL 4 (ANALYSIS)

* Identify an event in the story that could not happen in real life.

* Rumplestiltskin demands certain things from the girl, in return for the favors he did. What demands would you make if you were to do a favor for a friend?

* Identify an event in the story that you wish would happen to you.

LEVEL 5 (SYNTHESIS)

* Create a new ending telling what might happen if the queen could not guess Rumplestiltskin's name.

* Decide how the story would have been different if the miller had not told the king that his daughter could spin straw into gold.

* Create a new ending for the story telling what would happen if Rumplestiltskin never appeared to help the girl.

LEVEL 6 (EVALUATION)

* Judge whether the miller was a good father. Explain.

* List two ways in which Rumplestiltskin showed himself to be "good," and two ways in which he was "bad."

* Choose the character you would most like to meet. Explain.

THE SLEEPING BEAUTY

Brothers Grimm
Harcourt, Brace & Jovanovich
N.Y., 1959

In this well-known fairy tale, an angry fairy puts a spell on a beautiful princess that will cause her to die by pricking her finger on a spinning wheel. Another fairy modifies this spell and the princess and all the occupants of the castle fall asleep for one hundred years. A handsome prince awakens her and they all live happily ever after!

LEVEL 1 (KNOWLEDGE)

* What is the curse of the bad fairy?

* Identify the members of Sleeping Beauty's family.

* Name some of the gifts given by the good fairies.

LEVEL 2 (COMPREHENSION)

* Explain why everyone in the castle went to sleep.

* Describe the events in the story that took place after the princess fell asleep.

* Explain how the curse of the bad fairy was changed.

LEVEL 3 (APPLICATION)

* Decide what you would have given the princess as a gift if you were the fairy who had not been invited to the party.

* Think of something you did when you weren't invited to a party.

* Make use of information from the story to build a diorama showing your favorite scene.

LEVEL 4 (ANALYSIS)

* Identify some daily activities in the life of a princess.

* Categorize the events in the story. Describe those that are real and those that are imaginary.

* Compare Sleeping Beauty with Cinderella. How are they alike? How are they different?

LEVEL 5 (SYNTHESIS)

* How would the story be different if the King and Queen had not angered the bad fairy?

* Create a new ending for the story. Imagine that the Sleeping Beauty did not want to marry the Prince.

* Change the story so that the Princess does not prick her fingers on the spindle.

LEVEL 6 (EVALUATION)

* List five things you would do if you were a princess. Rank them in order of preference.

* Evaluate the behavior of the fairy who was not invited to the party.

* Choose the character in the story that you would like to be. Why?

HANSEL & GRETEL

Brothers Grimm
Alfred H. Knopf, N.Y., 1944

This familiar tale tells the story of a brother and sister who have to overcome many obstacles to stay alive. They finally conquer the witch and return home.

LEVEL 1 (KNOWLEDGE)

* Why were Hansel and Gretel left in the forest?

* Tell what plans Hansel made for finding the way home.

* Who owned the Gingerbread House?

LEVEL 2 (COMPREHENSION)

* Explain why the witch lived in a house covered with candy.

* Why did Gretel tell the witch that she didn't know how to check the oven?

* Describe what happened the second time the children were left in the woods.

LEVEL 3 (APPLICATION)

* Relate the mistake Hansel made on the second trip to the forest. Choose a better way for him to have found the path home.

* Decide how you would treat the children who came to your house if you were a witch.

* Build a model of the witch's house.

LEVEL 4 (ANALYSIS)

* Identify an event in the story that you would not like to happen to you. Identify one that you wish would happen.

* Analyze the witch's thoughts as she fed Hansel and Gretel.

* Think of a witch in another story you know. Compare the actions of the witch in *Hansel and Gretel* with those of the other witch.

LEVEL 5 (SYNTHESIS)

* Create other plans that Hansel and Gretel could have utilized in order to find their way back home.

* Retell the story, having Hansel and Gretel find an empty house in the forest instead of the witch's house.

* Develop other ways for Hansel and Gretel to stop the witch from hurting children.

LEVEL 6 (EVALUATION)

* Evaluate the father's actions. Was he a good father? Was he a good husband?

* Judge who you feel was the most clever character.

* Recall all the step-mothers you have read about. Rank in order of the kindest to the most cruel. Give reasons why the step-mothers in fairy tales behave as they do.

SYLVESTER, THE MOUSE WITH THE MUSICAL EAR

Adelaide Holl
Western Pub. Co., 1961

Sylvester is broken-hearted over leaving his country home where he hears music all day long. In the city, he finds solace inside a guitar in a music store. He then meets a musical cowboy named Tex.

LEVEL 1 (KNOWLEDGE)

* When the story begins, where does Sylvester live?

* Tell what happened to Sylvester's home.

* Who finally bought the "magic" guitar?

LEVEL 2 (COMPREHENSION)

* Why was Sylvester so happy when he found the guitar?

* Explain why people thought that the guitar was "magic."

* Offer three reasons why Sylvester and Tex liked each other immediately.

LEVEL 3 (APPLICATION)

* Choose a place in your house that might have made a nice home for Sylvester.

* Make a list of all the animals that needed to find a new home when your house was built.

* Think of ways that Sylvester could have stayed in his old home even after the bulldozers dug it up.

LEVEL 4 (ANALYSIS)

* Identify the things Sylvester might have liked about living in the guitar. Identify those things that he might not have liked.

* Compare Sylvester's life as a country mouse with his new life with Tex.

LEVEL 5 (SYNTHESIS)

* Create a story that describes Sylvester's adventures with Tex.

* Invent a musical instrument that can play by itself.

LEVEL 6 (EVALUATION)

* Decide whether Sylvester really had a musical ear. Explain.

* Judge whether Sylvester and Tex will be happy together. Give reasons for your answer.

* Choose one place in the story where you would like to live. Explain.

A BIRTHDAY FOR FRANCES

Russell Hoban
Harper & Row, N.Y., 1968

Jealous Frances turns her back on all the preparations for her sister Gloria's birthday party. Now, she feels even more left out. Mother Badger patienty waits until Frances thinks of buying Gloria a present with her own money. Father Badger offers to take care of the gift candy after half of it is eaten by Frances! At the party, Frances' generosity overrules her jealousy, and she and Gloria share good feelings.

LEVEL 1 (KNOWLEDGE)

* List the guests at Gloria's birthday party.

* Tell what Frances got Gloria for her birthday.

* Repeat Gloria's birthday wish.

LEVEL 2 (COMPREHENSION)

* Explain why Frances needed an imaginary friend.

* Tell why Frances and Albert were angry about having little sisters.

* Explain why Frances wouldn't sing "Happy Birthday" to Gloria.

LEVEL 3 (APPLICATION)

* Describe how you feel when your sister or brother has a birthday party.

* Think of what you would have bought as a present for your little sister if you were Frances.

* Draw a picture of something Frances might want for a birthday present.

LEVEL 4 (ANALYSIS)

* Analyze Frances' thoughts as Gloria made her birthday wish.

* Compare Frances' behavior toward Gloria with your own towards your sister, brother or friend who is the birthday boy or girl.

* Identify a person in the story that you can compare with someone you know.

LEVEL 5 (SYNTHESIS)

* Change the story by telling what would happen if Frances had eaten all of Gloria's presents.

* Even though Frances is a badger, the story is told as though she is a human child. Suppose you were planning a party for a real badger. Tell about the gifts you might give. Plan a party for each of the following: a dog, an ant, a lion, a parrot.

* Change the story, telling what would happen if Frances could not get her extra allowance money to buy Gloria's presents.

LEVEL 6 (EVALUATION)

* Evaluate the actions of Frances' parents. How did they show understanding towards their children?

* Judge which child reminded you of yourself. Tell why.

* Tell one way that Frances showed herself to be a "good" sister. Tell one way that she did not.

THE PIED PIPER

Joseph Jacobs
Cromwell Pub, N.Y., 1978

As though summoned through some magical powers, the Pied Piper appears in Hamlin and rids the town of its rats. However, the Mayor refuses to pay him what he had promised. As a result, the piper's tune leads the children out of Hamlin forever.

LEVEL 1 (KNOWLEDGE)

* Tell what the Piper did for Hamlin.

* Why were the people of Hamlin unhappy?

* Tell what the Piper did as his revenge against the Mayor.

LEVEL 2 (COMPREHENSION)

* Why did the Piper become angry?

* Explain why the rats followed the Piper.

* Describe how the Piper led the rats out of Hamlin.

LEVEL 3 (APPLICATION)

* How would you have treated the Piper if you were Mayor?

* Think of something you might ask the Piper to lead out of your house or town.

* Tell the story as though you are the child who is left behind at the end.

LEVEL 4 (ANALYSIS)

* Decide what parts of the story could happen today.

* Find parts of the story that suggest it was written a long time ago.

* What parts of the story suggest that it is a fairy tale?

LEVEL 5 (SYNTHESIS)

* Develop a new ending for the story. Assume the Piper gets his gold pieces.

* Think of different ways that the Piper could have reacted to the Mayor's refusal to pay him.

* Imagine what you would find in the place where the Piper led the children.

LEVEL 6 (EVALUATION)

* Choose the person who you think behaved most unfairly.

* List the characters that you thought were "good" and those that were not. Explain.

* Decide what you would have done if you were a child listening to the Piper's tune. Would you have followed him or stayed at home?

THE STORY OF FERDINAND

Munro Leaf
Viking Press, N.Y., 1936

Ferdinand is a peace-loving bull. He prefers smelling flowers to making a reputation for himself in the bullring.

LEVEL 1 (KNOWLEDGE)

* Who was Ferdinand?

* Where did Ferdinand live?

* Describe Ferdinand's favorite hobby.

LEVEL 2 (COMPREHENSION)

* Explain the problems Ferdinand had as a bull.

* Retell Ferdinand's experience at the bullfight from Ferdinand's point of view.

* Why was Ferdinand chosen to go to the bullfight?

LEVEL 3 (APPLICATION)

* Think of an animal that Ferdinand would rather have been.

* How would you have acted in Ferdinand's place?

* Find a photograph of a bullfight and compare it to Ferdinand's experience.

LEVEL 4 (ANALYSIS)

* Identify the events in the story that could really happen.

* Compare a bullfight to a boxing match. How are they alike? How are they different?

* Contrast Ferdinand's daily activities with those of the other bulls.

LEVEL 5 (SYNTHESIS)

* Create a new kind of bullfight where no one would get hurt. Describe it.

* Suppose Ferdinand *had* fought with the matador. Make up a new ending for the story.

* Imagine some activities that Ferdinand might like to do. Pantomime these for your classmates. Have them guess the activity.

LEVEL 6 (EVALUATION)

* Award first prize to the most understanding character in this story. Explain your choice.

* Evaluate the actions of Ferdinand's mother. Decide whether they are similar to or different from your mother's actions.

* Decide whether bullfighting is a good sport. Explain your answer.

BINKY BROTHERS DETECTIVES

James Lawrence
Harper and Row, N.Y., 1968

The story is about two brothers, Pinky and Dinky, who are detectives. They are hired by a baseball team to find a missing baseball mitt. While trying to solve the case, they experience many unusual and funny things.

LEVEL 1 (KNOWLEDGE)

* Name the two baseball teams.

* Why was Chub Doolin upset?

* Where did Dinky think the other team had hidden the mitt?

LEVEL 2 (COMPREHENSION)

* Explain how Pinky and Dinky got their nicknames.

* How did Dinky use Pink's predicament to his own advantage?

* Why did the Wildcats drop their "note" at the lemonade stand?

LEVEL 3 (APPLICATION)

* Demonstrate what you would have done at the lemonade stand if you were Pinky.

* Think of something that you misplaced or lost recently. Try to find it using the Binky Brothers' methods.

* Tell the story from the Wildcats' point of view.

LEVEL 4 (ANALYSIS)

* Examine the methods the Binky Brothers used to solve their problem. Group them into "things a good detective would do," and "things a good detective would not do."

* Compare Dinky to your own younger brother or sister. How are they alike? How are they different?

* Identify events in the story that have happened to you.

LEVEL 5 (SYNTHESIS)

* What if Dinky hadn't come along when Pinky was stuck in the tree house? Create a new ending.

* Design a tree house with several exits to the ground.

* Suppose the Binky Brothers were not able to solve the case. What would have happened?

LEVEL 6 (EVALUATION)

* List five qualities a detective should have. Decide whether Pinky and/or Dinky possess any or all of these qualities.

* Judge who the better detective was: Pinky or Dinky. Why?

* Select the one you feel was more clever: the Wildcats' trick or the Binky Brothers' solution. Explain your choice.

FROG AND TOAD TOGETHER

Arnold Lobel
Harper & Row, N.Y., 1972

Each of these five easy-to-read stories depicts the enduring quality of the friendship between Frog and Toad. Their adventures together demonstrate the joys of having one special friend.

LEVEL 1 (KNOWLEDGE)

* Name the activities on Toad's *List of things to do today.*

* Recall all the things Toad did to help his garden grow.

* Tell about Toad's dream.

LEVEL 2 (COMPREHENSION)

* Why wouldn't Toad run after his list as it blew away?

* Offer two reasons why Frog decided to give away the cookies to the birds.

* Explain why Toad was upset by his dream.

LEVEL 3 (APPLICATION)

* Interview Toad to find out why he likes Frog. Do the same with Frog.

* Record name(s) of your close friend(s) and list one thing that makes you want to be with that person.

* Prepare a filmstrip entitled, "A Day With Frog and Toad."

LEVEL 4 (ANALYSIS)

* Compare and contrast the personalities of Frog and Toad.

* Identify a part of the story that indicates how Toad feels about Frog.

* List some adventures of Frog and Toad that have also happened to you.

LEVEL 5 (SYNTHESIS)

* Suppose that Toad's dream grew into reality, and he became a superhero, **SUPERTOAD!** Write a story describing some events that might happen in his life.

* Make a *List of things to do today* for yourself. Try to follow it as closely as Toad did. Tell about your day. Imagine that you had to live that way.

* Discuss alternative ways for Frog and Toad to solve their problem with the cookies.

LEVEL 6 (EVALUATION)

* Judge whether Frog and Toad were brave. Explain your answer.

* Think of some qualities that a good friend might have. Evaluate Frog and Toad as friends.

* "Frog and Toad have more exciting lives than I do." Decide whether the statement is true or false. Explain.

ARROW TO THE SUN

Gerald McDermott
Holt, Rhinehart & Winston

The Boy, fatherless and friendless, goes to the Sun to find his father. After completing various trials of endurance, he returns to Earth as a man.

LEVEL 1 (KNOWLEDGE)

* Tell how the Boy came to be.

* State the reason why the other children would not befriend him.

* Who helped the Boy fly to the sun?

LEVEL 2 (COMPREHENSION)

* Explain why the Boy wanted to find his father.

* Why did the Boy have to pass through the trials?

* Draw a picture showing all the trials through which the Boy had to pass.

LEVEL 3 (APPLICATION)

* Think of something you might have to do to prove you are your father's son or daughter. Compare this to the Boy's tests.

* Draw a picture showing a trial through which you would have asked the Boy to pass.

* Imagine that you are a Pueblo Indian boy and you have found your father on the Sun. Paint a picture of him.

LEVEL 4 (ANALYSIS)

* Discover the things that make this story a "legend."

* Identify some Indian beliefs or superstitions.

* Analyze the thoughts the Boy might have had as an arrow journeying to the sun.

LEVEL 5 (SYNTHESIS)

* Design four new trials that would be most difficult for you if you were the Boy.

* Imagine how the story would change if the other children had made friends with the Boy.

* Create a new ending for the story. Assume that the Boy failed at one or more trials.

LEVEL 6 (EVALUATION)

* Determine which trial was the most difficult, and which was the easiest. Tell why.

* Judge whether the Boy was brave. Explain.

* Evaluate the Boy's character by listing five traits you feel he possessed. Rank them in order of importance to you.

THE MAGIC TREE

Gerald McDermott
Holt, Rhinehart & Winston, 1973

Mavungu leaves an unhappy family life and finds a wonderful new home. However, because he cannot keep his promise of secrecy, he loses all.

LEVEL 1 (KNOWLEDGE)

* Why did Mavungu leave home?

* Retell what happened when Mavungu pulled the leaves of the thick tree.

* Tell about the promise Mavungu made to the princess.

LEVEL 2 (COMPREHENSION)

* Explain why the village had disappeared when Mavungu returned.

* Offer two reasons why Mavungu broke his promise to the princess.

* Draw a picture of Mavungu before he met the princess and another showing what he looked like after she changed him.

LEVEL 3 (APPLICATION)

* If you were Mavungu, what would you have done when your mother questioned you about your new life?

* Construct a diorama of the village created by the princess.

* Relate the story from the point of view of Mavungu's mother.

LEVEL 4 (ANALYSIS)

* Identify the events in the story that indicate how Mavungu felt about his family.

* Compare the princess in this story to the fairy in "The Three Wishes."

* Describe an event in this story that you would like to have happen to you.

LEVEL 5 (SYNTHESIS)

* Suppose that Mavungu did not tell his mother the secret. Create a new ending for the story.

* Pretend Mavungu was a woman. How would the story change?

* Suppose the princess was angry at Mavungu for releasing her people from the Magic Tree. Make up a story telling what she might have done to him then.

LEVEL 6 (EVALUATION)

* Evaluate the punishment Mavungu received for breaking his promise. Do you consider it fair or unfair?

* Choose the character you would like to be. Explain your choice.

* Judge whether Mavungu's mother was a good parent. Explain.

AMELIA BEDELIA

Peggy Parish
Harper & Row, N.Y., 1963

Amelia Bedelia is a maid whose incredible talent for interpreting instructions, literally, results in comical situations.

LEVEL 1 (KNOWLEDGE)

* What was Amelia Bedelia's job?

* What did Amelia Bedelia do when she was asked to dust the furniture? Draw the drapes when the sun comes in? Dress the chicken?

* For whom did Amelia Bedelia work?

LEVEL 2 (COMPREHENSION)

* Explain why Amelia Bedelia had problems following directions.

* Draw a picture of the Rogers' house based on information from the story.

* Give two reasons why Mr. and Mrs. Rogers did not fire Amelia Bedelia.

LEVEL 3 (APPLICATION)

* Tell the story from the point of view of Mrs. Rogers.

* Put together a list of jobs for Amelia Bedelia to do at your house. Be careful how you word your directions!

* Interview Amelia Bedelia to find out why she interprets directions in such an unusual way.

LEVEL 4 (ANALYSIS)

* Compare Amelia Bedelia's style of living to that of Mr. and Mrs. Rogers. Think of one word to describe Amelia Bedelia and one word to describe the Rogers.

* Identify the point at which Mrs. Rogers became the angriest.

* Analyze Amelia Bedelia's thoughts as she followed the directions Mrs. Rogers left her.

LEVEL 5 (SYNTHESIS)

* Suppose Amelia Bedelia had not baked the wonderful pie. What might have happened to her?

* Create a new adventure for Amelia Bedelia. Be sure to include directions for her to follow in her own way.

* What if Amelia Bedelia were the kind of person to follow directions exactly? Describe her first day at the Rogers' house.

LEVEL 6 (EVALUATION)

* Judge whether Amelia Bedelia was a good housekeeper. Explain.

* Decide whether Mr. and Mrs. Rogers made the right decision in keeping Amelia Bedelia.

* Choose the person with whom you would have the most in common: Amelia Bedelia, Mr. Rogers or Mrs. Rogers. Explain.

I WISH LAURA'S MOMMY WAS MY MOMMY

Barbara Power
Lippincott, N.Y., 1979

Jennifer loves to visit Laura because Laura's Mommy gives her wonderful snacks, is patient and neat. When Jennifer's mother goes to work and Laura's mother becomes her babysitter on a regular basis, Jennifer begins to understand her own mother more and develops an appreciation for her own family.

LEVEL 1 (KNOWLEDGE)

* Tell what Jennifer and Laura did at Laura's house.

* List two things Laura learned from Jennifer and her family.

* Why did Jennifer wish Laura's mother could be her mother?

LEVEL 2 (COMPREHENSION)

* Explain why Jennifer's mother gave the children fruit or graham crackers as a snack.

* Why did Jennifer suggest that Laura's mother be their babysitter?

* Give reasons why Laura's mother began to ask her family for help around the house.

LEVEL 3 (APPLICATION)

* Interview Jennifer's mother and Laura's mother to find out how they spend their day.

* If you were Jennifer, how would you have felt about your mother's going back to work?

* Make use of the illustrations in the book to help you draw a mural of Laura's family and home, and Jennifer's family and home.

LEVEL 4 (ANALYSIS)

* Identify those activities you would rather do at Laura's house, and those you would rather do at Jennifer's.

* Analyze Jennifer's feelings when her mother tells her she's going back to work.

* Compare a day at your house to a day at both Jennifer's and Laura's homes.

LEVEL 5 (SYNTHESIS)

* Create a model mother that always does what you want! Write a story telling all the things you would do today if that person were your mother.

* Change the story so that Laura's mother goes back to work. Act out a new ending for the story.

* Suppose the title of the story were "I Wish Laura's Daddy were my Daddy." Rewrite the story to fit the title.

LEVEL 6 (EVALUATION)

* Decide whether you would rather have Jennifer or Laura as a close friend. Explain.

* List five qualities that you feel a good mother should possess. Rank them in order of importance.

* Judge whether Laura's mother and/or Jennifer's mother qualify as good mothers, according to your list.

THE BLIND MEN AND THE ELEPHANT

Lillian Quigley
Scribner, N.Y., 1959

In this retelling of an Indian fable, six blind men cannot agree on a single description for an elephant. This underlines the moral that, "to get a true picture of the whole, one must include all of its parts."

LEVEL 1 (KNOWLEDGE)

* Where did the six blind men live?

* Who lived in the palace?

* Each blind man compared the elephant to a certain object. List the objects.

LEVEL 2 (COMPREHENSION)

* Explain why each of the blind men thought the elephant was a different object.

* How did the rajah solve the blind men's problem?

* Retell the important events in the story.

LEVEL 3 (APPLICATION)

* Draw a separate picture of each blind man's description of the elephant.

* Try to put together the pictures you drew for the above question. Have you made an elephant?

* Blindfold yourself and have someone give you a large object to touch. Experiment with your description for each part of the object.

LEVEL 4 (ANALYSIS)

* What part of the story led you to believe that the blind men would eventually learn what an elephant looks like?

* Compare the words that the blind men used to describe the elephant. Are they similar to yours?

* Contrast the thinking of the blind men with that of the rajah.

LEVEL 5 (SYNTHESIS)

* Suppose six deaf men wanted to know what a piano sounds like. Create a story telling how they could find out.

* Predict what the elephant will look like to the blind men.

* Describe various parts of your imaginary animal and see if others can recreate it.

LEVEL 6 (EVALUATION)

* Judge who was the most clever: the rajah or the blind men. Explain.

* Select the character you would want to be. Why?

* Evaluate each of the blind men's descriptions of the elephant. Choose one that you believe to be most accurate.

CURIOUS GEORGE

H. A. Ray
Houghton Mifflin, Boston, 1941

George, a small, inquisitive monkey, has a multitude of adventures as he becomes accustomed to city life before he goes to live at the zoo.

LEVEL 1 (KNOWLEDGE)

* Recall what George did when he discovered the man's hat.

* Describe three situations where George got himself in trouble.

* Tell how George escaped from prison.

LEVEL 2 (COMPREHENSION)

* Explain how George fell into the ocean during his trip to the states.

* What reasons can you offer for George getting himself into so much trouble?

* Predict what would have happened if George did not escape from prison.

LEVEL 3 (APPLICATION)

* Pretend you are in charge of capturing animals for various zoos. Relate some of your concerns and interests.

* Make a mural showing George's adventures.

* Tell the story of George's capture from his point of view.

LEVEL 4 (ANALYSIS)

* George got himself into several problem situations. Identify a situation that you think was especially difficult for George.

* Describe the relationship between George and the man in the yellow straw hat.

* Analyze the thoughts of the people standing below as George flew through the air holding the balloons.

LEVEL 5 (SYNTHESIS)

* Suppose that you were the person in charge of George's safety. What would you have done to make sure George didn't get himself into trouble?

* Discuss how George's life might have been different if he had been found by a family who lived in the country after he escaped from prison.

* Predict how George's experiences might have been different if he weren't so curious.

LEVEL 6 (EVALUATION)

* Evaluate the method used to capture George.

* Determine how George will adjust to being placed in a zoo.

* Judge whether George showed intelligence. Explain your answer.

THE WOLF WHO HAD A WONDERFUL DREAM

Anne Rockwell
Thomas Y. Crowell, N.Y., 1973

After having a wonderful dream about a delicious meal, the hungry wolf goes out looking for dinner, but is outwitted by all his potential victims. He goes home hungry, but this time he dreams about a different kind of meal.

LEVEL 1 (KNOWLEDGE)

* Describe the wolf's dream.

* List the foods that he found undesirable.

* Tell about the wolf's experiences with the piglets.

LEVEL 2 (COMPREHENSION)

* Explain why the horse asked the wolf to take the thorn out of his foot.

* Retell the story from the point of view of the horse.

* Why did the wolf dream about the apple, bread and cheese in his second dream?

LEVEL 3 (APPLICATION)

* Interview the wolf at the end of his day and report to the class how he feels.

* If you were the wolf, what plan would you have made for catching the piglets?

* Name several things the wolf would have enjoyed eating at your house.

LEVEL 4 (ANALYSIS)

* Wolves in stories are often villains, capable of all sorts of trickery. State the ways in which this wolf is similiar to wolves in other familiar stories. State ways in which he is different.

* Identify parts of the story that you thought might have ended differently.

* What parts of the story made you feel sorry for the wolf?

LEVEL 5 (SYNTHESIS)

* Suppose you were the wolf. Tell a story describing your dream.

* Imagine what might have happened if the wolf had not washed the piglets.

* Create a "wonderful dream" for the pig.

LEVEL 6 (EVALUATION)

* Judge the success of the wolf in this story as compared to that of the wolf in "Little Red Riding Hood."

* Who do you think was the most clever character in the story and why?

* Evaluate the wisdom of the wolf's decision.

SYLVESTER AND THE MAGIC PEBBLE

Williiam Steig
Simon and Schuster

Sylvester, a very human donkey, finds a magic pebble and he turns himself into a rock before he realizes the consequences. His parents mourn for him, thinking he will never be seen again, as he spends season after season wishing to turn back into a donkey. Finally, springtime comes and his parents have a picnic on the rock that is Sylvester! When they find the magic pebble and place it on Sylvester, he is able to turn himself back into a donkey again.

LEVEL 1 (KNOWLEDGE)

* Describe the pebble found by Sylvester.

* Recall the first event that made Sylvester think that the pebble might have magical powers.

* How did Sylvester become a donkey again?

LEVEL 2 (COMPREHENSION)

* Explain why Sylvester could not change back into a donkey after he had turned himself into a rock.

* Offer two reasons why the Duncans decided to go on a picnic.

* Why did Sylvester put the magic pebble in a safe?

LEVEL 3 (APPLICATION)

* Choose ways that you might have protected yourself from the lion.

* Prepare a filmstrip (mural) showing Sylvester's experiences in this story.

* Interview Sylvester's parents before they leave for the picnic and after they return.

LEVEL 4 (ANALYSIS)

* Analyze Sylvester's feelings as he remains a rock and the seasons come and go.

* Compare Sylvester's experiences with the magic beans.(See *Jack and the Beanstalk.*)

* Identify ways in which Mr. and Mrs. Duncan are like your parents. In what ways are they different?

LEVEL 5 (SYNTHESIS)

* Suppose Sylvester's parents did not go on the picnic. Imagine other ways that Sylvester might have turned back into himself.

* Tell how Sylvester's experiences might have been different if he had changed himself into: a fish, an elephant, a bee, a dinosaur.

* Predict some new hobbies for Sylvester after his safe return home.

LEVEL 6 (EVALUATION)

* Evaluate Sylvester's use of the magic pebble; did he use it wisely?

* Judge whether Mr. and Mrs. Duncan were good parents. Explain.

* Decide which character you would most like to be. Give reasons.

WHAT MARY JO SHARED

Janice May Udry
Albert Whitman, N.Y., 1966

Whenever Mary Jo selects something for show and tell, one of her classmates has already chosen it. Finally, she brings a very special person to share with the class: her father.

LEVEL 1 (KNOWLEDGE)

* List the things Mary Jo first thought about sharing.

* Explain why Mary Jo did not share these things.

* Tell what Mary Jo shared.

LEVEL 2 (COMPREHENSION)

* Summarize the story.

* Explain why Mary Jo asked her father to come to school with her.

* Why were the children suddenly interested in talking about their fathers?

LEVEL 3 (APPLICATION)

* Select something unusual that you might bring to school to share.

* Introduce your father, mother or another relative to the class.

* Use information from the story to list the things you know about Mary Jo's father.

LEVEL 4 (ANALYSIS)

* Identify the things your father has in common with Mary Jo's father.

* Identify the things that make your father different from Mary Jo's father.

* Have you ever felt shy about sharing something with your class? Compare your experience with Mary Jo's father.

LEVEL 5 (SYNTHESIS)

* Suppose Mary Jo's father couldn't come to school that day. Think of something unusual that Mary Jo could have shared instead.

* Create a "Share Your Family Day" at school. Prepare three questions to ask each shared family member.

* Invent a pill to get rid of shyness, and try it out on a shy person in your class! See if you can make this person your friend.

LEVEL 6 (EVALUATION)

* Judge whether Mary Jo shared something that no one else had thought of before.

* Choose a character in the story whom you would like to know.

* Give a "Father of the Year" award to a storybook father. Explain your choice.

ALEXANDER & THE TERRIBLE, HORRIBLE, NO GOOD, VERY BAD DAY

Judith Viorst
Atheneum, N.Y., 1972

Alexander knows right from the start that it is going to be a very bad day. Absolutely nothing goes right, and he considers moving to Australia! It makes him feel better when his mother reassures him that some days are like that for everyone.

LEVEL 1 (KNOWLEDGE)

* Who is Alexander?

* When did Alexander first know it was going to be a "terrible horrible, no good, very bad day?"

* Tell about some of the events that ruined Alexander's day.

LEVEL 2 (COMPREHENSION)

* Explain why Alexander talked about going to Australia.

* Arrange the events that made Alexander's day terrible in the order in which they took place.

* Why might Mrs. Dickens have preferred Paul's picture of the sailboat to Alexander's picture of the invisible castle?

LEVEL 3 (APPLICATION)

* Try to think of ways that Alexander could have improved his day.

* Use information from the story to create a puppet show about Alexander.

* What could you have done to help Alexander have a better day?

LEVEL 4 (ANALYSIS)

* Compare Alexander's day to the wolf's day in the story *The Wolf Had a Wonderful Dream*. How were they alike? How were they different?

* Identify events in the story that have happened to you.

* Discover as many clues as possible in the story indicating that Alexander is a very young boy.

LEVEL 5 (SYNTHESIS)

* Suppose that Alexander could have one wish on his terrible day. Draw a picture showing what he would have wished for and tell how that might have affected the rest of his day.

* Act out a new story about Alexander and the "terrific, wonderful, very good fantastic day."

LEVEL 6 (EVALUATION)

* Choose what you believe to be the three worst things that happened to Alexander.

* Think about the last time you had a terrible day. Decide whose day was worse: yours or Alexander's. Why?

* Conclude whether Alexander's day was as miserable as the title of the book suggests.

82

THE LITTLE WITCH WANDA

Mariette Vanhalewin
World Publishing Company

*Wanda's mother, dismayed by her daughter's continuous dis-
obedience, leaves her among humans to perform a good deed.
Wanda's experience and feelings are explored as she wanders
alone in an unfamiliar place.*

LEVEL 1 (KNOWLEDGE)

* Where did Wanda go with Patsy?

* Tell about Wanda's punishment.

* Describe the good deed Wanda was able to do.

LEVEL 2 (COMPREHENSION)

* Explain why Wanda's mother was so angry with her behavior.

* Why did people think Wanda was a witch?

* Tell why Wanda's mother flew to Dindelord to take Wanda
  home.

LEVEL 3 (APPLICATION)

* Wanda was angry at her mother for not listening to her. Think
  of some things that you've done when you felt that your
  mother or father was too busy to listen to you.

* Make a list of "good deeds" that Wanda could have done.

* Decide how you would have treated Wanda if she had come
  to your house.

LEVEL 4 (ANALYSIS)

* Compare Wanda to another witch you have read about.

* Analyze Wanda's feelings as her mother left her near Dindelord.

* Identify the reasons that people were afraid of Wanda. Why wasn't the little boy afraid?

LEVEL 5 (SYNTHESIS)

* Suppose that Wanda were a Martian instead of a witch. Create a new story telling some of her adventures.

* What if the little boy were also a witch? Tell what might have happened.

* Imagine that you were a witch with magical powers. How would this affect your relationships with family, friends and teachers?

LEVEL 6 (EVALUATION)

* Evaluate Wanda's mother's choice of punishment.

* Decide which character you would most like to be. Why?

* Judge whether Wanda's mother was a good parent. Give reasons.

WILL YOU COUNT THE STARS WITHOUT ME?

Jane Breskin Zalbea
Farrar Straus, N.Y., 1979

Saba and Shana are two monkeys who have never been separated. When Shana has to go away to search for food, Saba is lost and forlorn. His friends begin to ask him to help them with their problems. When Shana returns, they both realize that they can exist independently, although they are happier together.

LEVEL 1 (KNOWLEDGE)

* Who were Saba and Shana?

* List their friends. What kind of animals were they?

* Recall all the things that Saba and Shana needed in order to make them happy.

LEVEL 2 (COMPREHENSION)

* Explain why Shana left.

* Tell ways in which Saba helped his friends and give reasons why they asked for help.

* Describe Saba's feelings when Shana went away.

LEVEL 3 (APPLICATION)

* Relate how you would have felt if you were Saba.

* Try to think of all the things you would do if you were left alone for a week.

* Make use of information about Saba's island and build a diorama.

LEVEL 4 (ANALYSIS)

* Compare Shana to Helga in the story *Helga's Dowry*. How are they alike? How are they different?

* Identify something in the story that you would have done if you were on Saba's island.

* Contrast Saba's feelings when Shana first left, with his feelings by the time she returned.

LEVEL 5 (SYNTHESIS)

* Suppose that Saba and Shana were a boy and a girl, respectively. Retell the story.

* Create a machine that could have gone to look for food in Shana's place. Explain how it would work.

* Change the story so that Saba goes to look for food. Tell what Shana might have done on their island.

LEVEL 6 (EVALUATION)

* Choose the character you would like to be. Explain your choice.

* Select the most clever animal in the story. Give reasons for your choice.

* Choose the animal you would like most to meet on a tropical island. Why?

Chapter 3

IT'S SO NICE TO HAVE
A WOLF AROUND THE HOUSE

Harry Allard
Doubleday & Co., N.Y., 1977

The story is about a Wolf who comes to live with an old man and his three pets. It turns out that the Wolf was in trouble with the law and was looking for a place to hide. He is finally caught and brought to court. However, the old man has developed a strong relationship with the Wolf and pleads to the Judge for his release, on the basis of how much the Wolf has helped the old man.

LEVEL 1 (KNOWLEDGE)

* Identify the names of the three pets who lived with the old man.

* How did the old man get Cuthbert the Wolf to come to his house?

* What did the old man find out in the newspaper about Cuthbert the Wolf?

LEVEL 2 (COMPREHENSION)

* Describe what the Wolf did that pleased the three pets and the old man.

* Why did the Judge allow the Wolf to go free and remain with the old man?

* Explain the reason for the change in the pets' and the old man's behavior after the   wolf got sick.

LEVEL 3 (APPLICATION)

* If you wanted to have a charming companion, how would your family help you to get one?

* Suppose you, like the old man, had three pets. What might you do for them to make them happier, healthier and more alive?

* How else could the old man have advertised that he wanted a charming companion? What methods could he have used?

LEVEL 4 (ANALYSIS)

* Why did Cuthbert the Wolf want to live with the pets and the old man?

* Compare the behavior of the pets and the old man before and after the wolf became sick.

* Why did the pets forget about their aches and pains and become frisky again?

LEVEL 5 (SYNTHESIS)

* What might have happened to the pets and to the old man if the wolf had been mean and ferocious?

* Imagine that the Judge sent the Wolf to jail for the bank robberies. What do you suppose the pets and the old man would have done?

* Suppose Cuthbert had been a dog. Imagine Ginger's reaction when the dog came to the house to live.

LEVEL 6 (EVALUATION)

* What made the Judge free Cuthbert and allow him to remain with the old man and the three pets?

* If the old man had better eyesight and recognized that Cuthbert was a wolf, how might the old man have reacted?

* Do you think it is possible for a wolf to come and live with a family? Explain.

88

TWO HUNDRED RABBITS

Lonzo Anderson & Adrienne Adams
The Viking Press, N.Y., 1968

In the forest, a little boy meets an old lady who helps him make a magic whistle. The boy uses the whistle to march two hundred rabbits before the king during festival day.

LEVEL 1 (KNOWLEDGE)

* Where did the boy live?

* What did the old lady suggest the boy make in the forest?

* Why was the King not happy with the marching rabbits at first?

LEVEL 2 (COMPREHENSION)

* Describe two things that the boy practiced in the forest in preparation for the King's festival.

* Why did the rabbits follow the boy?

* How was the problem of the missing rabbit solved?

LEVEL 3 (APPLICATION)

* If you wanted to entertain the King on Festival Day, what might you do?

* Can you think of other animals that might have followed the boy in the parade?

* Show how the boy made a whistle from the branch of a Slipper-elm tree.

LEVEL 4 (ANALYSIS)

* How would you describe the old lady?

* How would you compare the marching rabbits with other events the King saw during the festival?

* What kind of relationship did the boy and the King have as a result of the boy's marching rabbit performances?

LEVEL 5 (SYNTHESIS)

* Suppose the boy blew his whistle and other animals came out of the woods. What kind of animals might have come, and how would the boy have handled the situation?

* Create a different ending to the story. Imagine that the King was very angry about the marching rabbits.

* What else do you suppose the old lady could have done for the boy with her magical power?

LEVEL 6 (EVALUATION)

* Describe what would have happened if the rabbits decided to run wildly through crowds of people.

* Judge what the King would have done if the two hundredth (last) rabbit didn't appear.

* What do you suppose might happen if the boy were to meet the old lady again? Explain.

THERE'S NOTHING TO DO, SO. . .
LET ME BE YOU

Jean Horton Berg
West Minister Press, 1966

The story is about a Baby Raccoon who can't find anything to do except come into the house and say to his parents, "there's nothing to do." Baby Raccoon's parents then suggest that he pretend to be Mother Raccoon and do the everyday chores around the house. This includes washing dishes, dusting, etc. While playing Mother Raccoon, Baby Raccoon experiences a lot of difficulty. His parents decide to come into the house saying, "there's nothing to do."

LEVEL 1 (KNOWLEDGE)

* With whom did Mother Raccoon suggest Baby Raccoon play?

* List the things Baby Raccoon did in the house while playing the role of Mother Raccoon.

* What did Baby Raccoon tell his parents to go outside to do?

LEVEL 2 (COMPREHENSION)

* Explain what happened when Baby Raccoon began to wash the dishes.

* What did Baby Raccoon do after he finished sweeping the kitchen floor?

* Describe what was said during the peanut butter sandwich lunch.

LEVEL 3 (APPLICATION)

* How often do you come into the house and say "I have nothing to do?"

91

* Would your mother let you pretend to be mother? If so, what would she let you do?

* If you dropped a plate on the floor and it smashed into many little pieces, how would you go about cleaning up the mess?

LEVEL 4 (ANALYSIS)

* Why do you think Mother Raccoon let Baby Raccoon take over her jobs in the house?

* Compare Baby Raccoon's tasks while playing mother. What did he have to do as a Baby Raccoon? Which was more difficult? Why?

* Why do you think Mother and Father Raccoon kept coming into the house and saying they had nothing to do?

LEVEL 5 (SYNTHESIS)

* Imagine that Baby Raccoon had to be a Mother Raccoon for a very long time. How do you think he would have liked it?

* Create other problems which Baby Raccoon might have experienced while playing Mother Raccoon.

* Suppose your mother allowed you to change roles with her for a day. How would you go about planning the day?

LEVEL 6 (EVALUATION)

* Describe how Mother and Father Raccoon felt having Baby Raccoon working inside the house all day.

* Do you think it is a good idea for children to play Mother and Father roles once in a while? If so, why?

* How would you judge the kind of job Baby Raccoon did in the house while playing Mother Raccoon?

THE ACCIDENT

Carol Carrick
The Seabury Press, N.Y., 1976

While walking along a dark road, a little boy's dog is hit by a truck.

LEVEL 1 (KNOWLEDGE)

* Why didn't Christopher go with his parents for a canoe ride?

* Where did Christopher and Bodger want to go after the television show was over?

* What happened to Bodger on the way to the lake?

LEVEL 2 (COMPREHENSION)

* Describe how Bodger got hit by a car.

* Explain what the man said to Christopher after he hit Bodger.

* Where did Christopher's father bury Bodger?

LEVEL 3 (APPLICATION)

* What did Christopher learn from this bad experience?

* Could Christopher have prevented the accident? How?

* How else might Bodger have been involved in an accident?

LEVEL 4 (ANALYSIS)

* Why was Bodger walking on the other side of the road when the truck came along?

* Compare the feelings of the truck driver to those of Christopher's father concerning the loss of Bodger.

* How would you describe Christopher's feelings about the loss of Bodger?

LEVEL 5 (SYNTHESIS)

* Suppose the truck had only injured Bodger. What would Christopher and his family have done for Bodger right after the accident?

* What other accidents might have occurred as Christopher and Bodger went looking for his parents at the lake?

* Create a new ending to the story.

LEVEL 6 (EVALUATION)

* What might the truck driver do for Christopher as a way of saying he is sorry?

* Judge whether or not the truck driver should have seen Bodger in time to avoid hitting the dog.

* Decide what Christopher will do to replace Bodger.

MARTHA ANN & THE MOTHER STORE

Nathaniel and Betty Jo Charnley
Harcourt, Brace & Jovanovich, N.Y., 1973

A little girl named Martha Ann is unhappy with her mother. She takes her to a Mother Store to find a new mother. After trying several different mothers, Martha Ann decides that nobody can be perfect and that she really loves her mother.

LEVEL 1 (KNOWLEDGE)

* What is the little girl's name?

* Where did she take her mother?

* How many mothers did Martha Ann try?

LEVEL 2 (COMPREHENSION)

* Why did Martha Ann take her mother to the Mother Store?

* What did she like/dislike about the other mothers?

* Explain why Martha Ann was angry.

LEVEL 3 (APPLICATION)

* What do you dislike about your mother?

* Have you ever found yourself in a similiar situation?

* Show how changes in behavior could resolve the conflict.

LEVEL 4 (ANALYSIS)

* Compare Martha Ann's relationship with each of the other mothers.

* What characteristics of the other mothers did Martha Ann like?

* How did Martha Ann's mother differ from the other mothers?

LEVEL 5 (SYNTHESIS)

* What would you have done if you were Martha Ann?

* Pretend you were a salesperson in the Mother Store. How would you help Martha Ann select a perfect mother?

* What sort of a child would your parents select, if they could go to a children's store?

LEVEL 6 (EVALUATION)

* Do you think Martha Ann made the right decision at the end? Why?

* Describe the qualities you would look for in the perfect mother.

* Judge how Martha Ann's mother felt about the possibility of being replaced.

NOTHING MUCH HAPPENED TODAY

Mary Blount Christian
Addison-Wesley Publishing, 1973.

The story is about three children who were left home alone for twenty minutes while their mother went shopping. During that time, a robber and a policeman came running through their house causing a big mess. When mother returned home, she couldn't believe all that had happened to her children and to her house.

LEVEL 1 (KNOWLEDGE)

* When Mrs. Maeberry returned home from shopping, what was the first thing she noticed about her house?

* What were the pets' names?

* How long was Mrs. Maeberry gone from the house?

LEVEL 2 (COMPREHENSION)

* Explain why there were bubbles floating everywhere.

* Describe what event started the whole mess.

* Can you describe all the things that happened to the children while Mrs. Maeberry was gone?

LEVEL 3 (APPLICATION)

* If you had a dog who got sugar all over herself, what would you do?

* If your mother came home and found such a big mess, how do you think she would have reacted?

* What would you have done if a robber and a policeman came running through your house?

LEVEL 4 (ANALYSIS)

* Why do you think the spilled cake batter caused the oven to smoke?

* What thoughts do you suppose the children had as the robber was running through their house?

* Do you think it is possible for all those things to happen to the children in only twenty minutes?

LEVEL 5 (SYNTHESIS)

* Suppose the robber came running into Mrs. Maeberry's house and there wasn't a policeman chasing him. Would this have created a different set of events?

* Think of other things that could have happened in the house while the robber was being chased.

* How else might Mrs. Maeberry have reacted when she heard what had happened to her children?

LEVEL 6 (EVALUATION)

* Why did the robber decide to run into Mrs. Maeberry's house?

* If the smoke coming from the oven had continued, what would have happened?

* When Mr. Maeberry came home that night, what do you think were his reactions to the events of the day?

LISA & THE GROMPET

Patricia Coombs
Lothrop, Lee & Shepard Co., N.Y., 1970

A little girl named Lisa runs away from her home because of being told what to do. While going through the woods, Lisa meets a Grompet. The Grompet convinces Lisa to return home to her parents.

LEVEL 1 (KNOWLEDGE)

* Why did Lisa decide to leave home?

* Who did Lisa meet in the woods?

* What was the Grompet's uncle's name?

LEVEL 2 (COMPREHENSION)

* Name the things Lisa's family reminded her of each day.

* Describe how Lisa met the Grompet.

* What did Lisa do with the Grompet when she returned home?

LEVEL 3 (APPLICATION)

* What do your parents usually say when you get up in the morning?

* What did Lisa learn from this experience?

* Will Lisa tell her parents about the Grompet's story?

LEVEL 4 (ANALYSIS)

* Compare Lisa's story to the Grompet's story.

* What did Lisa say to the Grompet which made him so very happy?

* Why did Lisa want to return home after talking to the Grompet?

LEVEL 5 (SYNTHESIS)

* Imagine that Lisa hadn't met the Grompet and wandered further into the woods. What might have happened?

* Suppose Lisa had told her family how she felt about always being told what to do. How might her family have reacted?

* What can Lisa do so that her family doesn't always tell her everything to do? Devise a plan.

LEVEL 6 (EVALUATION)

* Describe how Lisa felt when she wandered through the woods.

* Judge how Lisa's mother would have felt if she had learned that Lisa had run away.

* What things does this story teach us about mothers and fathers and little children?

THE LOUDEST NOISE IN THE WORLD

Benjamin Elkin
The Viking Press, N.Y., 1954

A little Prince named Hulla-Baloo asks the King for a special birthday wish. The Prince wants to hear the loudest sound in the world. People all over the world prepare to yell on the day of the Prince's birthday. However, when the moment comes nobody yells. Complete silence is experienced.

LEVEL 1 (KNOWLEDGE)

* What was the name of the loudest city in the world?

* What did Prince Hulla-Baloo want for his birthday?

* What did people all over the world do when Prince Hulla-Baloo's "birthday moment" came?

LEVEL 2 (COMPREHENSION)

* Describe Prince Hulla-Baloo's favorite game.

* Why did people all over the world decide to remain silent?

* What did the Prince notice during the silence?

LEVEL 3 (APPLICATION)

* Describe things in your neighborhood which make a lot of noise.

* Is it possible to reduce the amount of noise in New York City? If so, how?

* How would your parents react if you wanted to make a lot of noise?

LEVEL 4 (ANALYSIS)

* How did all the people of the world know to be silent during the "birthday moment?"

* Why did Hub Bub have its city sign changed from "The Loudest" to "The Quietest City in the World?"

* How did the people of Hub Bub contribute toward making their city the loudest in the world?

LEVEL 5 (SYNTHESIS)

* Suppose you wanted to hear the loudest sound in the world for your birthday. Describe that sound.

* Suppose all the people of the world yelled during the "birthday moment." How would you describe the sound?

* Create other games Prince Hulla-Baloo could have played with his friends, which make a lot of noise.

LEVEL 6 (EVALUATION)

* How did people feel when the King asked everyone to yell on the Prince's birthday?

* Describe Prince Hulla-Baloo's feelings after he heard certain beautiful sounds during the moment of silence period.

* How do you think the people of Hub Bub felt about having a quiet city? Explain.

THE ISLAND OF THE SKOG

Steven Kellogg
The Dial Press, N.Y., 1973

Several mice, referred to as "rowdies," are dissatisfied with life in their present home. They decide to move and travel to the Island of the Skog. Many exciting things happen to the rowdies during their voyage and after they land on the island.

LEVEL 1 (KNOWLEDGE)

* Why did the mice decide to leave their home?

* Who was the leader of the rowdies?

* What did the rowdies have to eat on the ship?

LEVEL 2 (COMPREHENSION)

* Describe what their trip to the island was like.

* How did the rowdies trap the Skog?

* What did the Skog say to the rowdies after being captured?

LEVEL 3 (APPLICATION)

* How did the rowdies plan to solve the Skog problem?

* How else might the rowdies have caught the Skog?

* Would the rowdies have encountered a similar situation if they had gone to another island?

LEVEL 4 (ANALYSIS)

* Describe the events that happened to the rowdies which encouraged them to leave their home.

* Compare the different methods used by the rowdies to capture the Skog.

* Why was the rowdies' voyage to the island so difficult?

LEVEL 5 (SYNTHESIS)

* How would you have dealt with the threatening Skog situation?

* If the rowdies decided not to leave home, describe what they might have done to improve their living situation.

* Create a different Skog. Suppose this Skog didn't like the rowdies coming to the Island.

LEVEL 6 (EVALUATION)

* Why did the first two attempts to capture the Skog fail?

* What type of character was the Skog? Explain.

* Judge whether the rowdies made a good decision by going to the Island of the Skog. Explain.

DOOLY & THE SNORTSNOOT

Jack Kent
G. P. Putnam's Sons, N.Y., 1972

*A young giant named Dooly confronts the Snortsnoot monster.
Although Dooley is a small giant, he becomes huge as he success-
fully defends the other children from the Snortsnoot.*

LEVEL 1 (KNOWLEDGE)

* How did Dooly differ from his family?

* In what ways did Dooly differ from the other children?

* What did Dooly's mother feed Dooly to make him strong?

LEVEL 2 (COMPREHENSION)

* What do you think makes a giant feel more like a giant?

* What was the attitude of the other children toward Dooly?

* Describe the way in which Dooly saved Treena from the
  Snortsnoot.

LEVEL 3 (APPLICATION)

* In what ways does physical appearance affect the way we
  perceive other people?

* "I think I just grew up because it was time to," said Dooly,
  modestly. How could this statement apply to you?

* How might Dooly have saved himself if he had not grown?

LEVEL 4 (ANALYSIS)

* Compare Dooly's attitude about himself to that which the other children had of him.

* What do you think caused Dooly to jump on the tail of the Snortsnoot?

* Compare Dooly before and after he met the Snortsnoot.

LEVEL 5 (SYNTHESIS)

* Why do you think Dooly grew so suddenly?

* Why did Dooly's clothing grow with him?

* Retell the story from the Snortsnoot's point of view.

LEVEL 6 (EVALUATION)

* What kind of a giant will Dooly make? Explain.

* How else was Dooly a giant besides being big?

* How will Dooly treat the other children, now that he has become a giant?

106

BUNYA THE WITCH

Robert Kraus and Mischa Richter
Windmill Books, N.Y., 1971

Bunya is the story of a witch with magical powers. The people of the village treat her unkindly and, as a result, are changed into frogs and pigs. Bunya finally turns the animals back to people and leaves the village.

LEVEL 1 (KNOWLEDGE)

* What did Bunya do to the children in the beginning of the story?

* What were the words Bunya used to turn the animals back into people?

* How did the story end?

LEVEL 2 (COMPREHENSION)

* Why did the children think Bunya was a witch?

* What happened when the frogs went home?

* How did the story end?

LEVEL 3 (APPLICATION)

* How would you have used Bunya's power?

* Show how you would act if you were to become a frog.

* How would your parents have acted if you had come home as a frog?

LEVEL 4 (ANALYSIS)

* Why didn't Bunya want the people to compliment her?

* Compare how the people in the story felt about Bunya at the beginning and at the end of the story.

* Why did the children believe that Bunya was a real witch?

LEVEL 5 (SYNTHESIS)

* Imagine what would happen if Bunya hadn't changed them back into people.

* What do you think Bunya will do with her new powers?

* Create a new ending to the story. Suppose the people were angry at Bunya. What might have happened?

LEVEL 6 (EVALUATION)

* Why do you think the authors selected frogs and pigs?

* Judge how Bunya felt when the children called her a witch.

* How will the people feel about Bunya if she decides to return to the village?

DRAGON STEW

Tom McGowen
Follett Pub., Ill., 1969

The story is about a king who loved to eat and, as a result was named King Chubby. The King fired all his cooks because they didn't want the king in their kitchen. After a great search, King Chubby finds a new royal cook named Klaus Binkelspiel.

LEVEL 1 (KNOWLEDGE)

* What was King Chubby's favorite hobby?

* What did King Chubby do in order to find a new royal cook?

* Name the unusual recipe described to the King.

LEVEL 2 (COMPREHENSION)

* Explain why all the King's cooks left the Castle.

* Describe the King's eating schedule.

* Why didn't Klaus Binkelspiel cook the Dragon?

LEVEL 3 (APPLICATION)

* If you were the King's doctor, how would you have advised him about his eating habits?

* How would you have selected a new royal cook?

* Suppose the King were coming to your house for dinner; how would you and your family have prepared for the visit?

LEVEL 4 (ANALYSIS)

* Why do you think the King wanted to be so involved in preparing food at the castle?

* Describe the relationship between the King and Klaus Binkelspiel.

* What thoughts do you suppose Klaus had when the soldiers brought the dragon to the kitchen to be prepared for cooking?

LEVEL 5 (SYNTHESIS)

* What might have happened to Klaus had he not been able to make the dragon stew which was promised to the King?

* Suppose the dragon was vicious and angry. Discuss how Klaus would have handled the situation.

* Create a new ending to the story. Imagine that the King didn't like dragon stew.

LEVEL 6 (EVALUATION)

* Judge whether you think the King was healthy.

* How would you describe the feelings of the village people towards King Chubby?

* What do you think would have happened had the King not met Klaus?

THE APPLE WAR

Bernice Myers
Parents' Magazine Press, N.Y.
1973

*Two Kings get into an argument and a possible war over the
location of an apple tree. Each King prepares for war; however,
they are spared this event because a mediator named William
solves the problem for the Kings.*

LEVEL 1 (KNOWLEDGE)

* Where was the apple tree located?

* Who were the main characters?

* What was the name of King Sam's advisor?

LEVEL 2 (COMPREHENSION)

* What was the argument about?

* What were the reasons for calling off the war?

* Describe the apple tree and where it was situated.

LEVEL 3 (APPLICATION)

* Discuss King Sam's inability to make a decision.

* What proof can you give that King Sam really didn't want a war?

* How would you attempt to prevent the Kings from arguing
about the apple tree?

111

LEVEL 4 (ANALYSIS)

* Compare how you might have handled the situation with the way King Sam handled it.

* Analyze King Oscar's feelings as he prepared for war.

* Why was William able to solve the problem?

LEVEL 5 (SYNTHESIS)

* Predict what would happen if this story continued.

* What if King Sam's birthday had not come? How do you suppose the war would have been stopped?

* Describe a current event which is similar to this story. Explain.

LEVEL 6 (EVALUATION)

* Determine what issues cause wars and explore ways by which these wars could have been   avoided.

* Choose instances in which a promise should not be kept and justify your answer.

* What do you think Oscar and Sam learned from this experience? Explain.

ELI

Bill Peet
Houghton Mifflin Co., Mass, 1978

*Eli is a lion who is old and not very confident about himself.
One day, some hunters came along and were about to find Eli.
However, some vultures protected Eli by pretending Eli was dead.
They pretended to feast on his remains. Eli was very grateful to
the vultures and began a friendly relationship with them.*

LEVEL 1 (KNOWLEDGE)

* How was Eli described in the beginning of the story?

* Tell what Eli did to become friendly with the vultures.

* Who was following Eli's trail?

LEVEL 2 (COMPREHENSION)

* Why did Eli raise his voice and call the vultures horrible names?

* Explain what the vultures did to protect Eli from the hunters.

* Describe the reactions of the hunters as they saw Eli lying
  beneath all the vultures.

LEVEL 3 (APPLICATION)

* Do you think the dogs could feel the way Eli felt about himself?

* Is it possible for birds to protect another animal as the vultures
  protected Eli?

* What other kinds of animals do hunters search for in the jungles?

LEVEL 4 (ANALYSIS)

* Why do you think Eli ran to help Vera the Vulture as she was being attacked by the jackal?

* Why was Eli at first annoyed at having the vultures sit over him in the trees?

* How would you describe the relationship between Eli and the vultures at the end of the story?

LEVEL 5 (SYNTHESIS)

* Suppose Eli was a mean, hungry lion. Would he have tried to save Vera the Vulture from being eaten by the jackal?

* Imagine that the hunters checked to see if Eli was really dead and found him to be very much alive. What might have happened?

* Create a new story using different animals.

LEVEL 6 (EVALUATION)

* When the other lions were having a feast and Eli watched, how do you think he felt about being left out?

* Do you think vultures or any other type of birds could possibly be kind to other animals and be able to show kindness through some action?

* Judge whether you think it is right for hunters to attack lions.

TIMOTHY'S FLOWER

Jean Van Leeuwen
Random House, N.Y., 1967

Timothy is a boy who lives in the city. One day, Timothy's grandmother took him to a park where he discovered beautiful flowers. Timothy brought some yellow flowers home and showed them to his neighbors. As a result, Timothy's relationship with Mrs. Valdez, a neighbor, was greatly enhanced.

LEVEL 1 (KNOWLEDGE)

* Name some of the people who lived on Timothy's block.

* What did Timothy find in the park and take home with him?

* How did Timothy almost lose his yellow flower?

LEVEL 2 (COMPREHENSION)

* Describe the park that Timothy and his grandmother visited.

* How did Mr. Pepperoni help Timothy?

* Explain Mrs. Valdez's feelings when she saw Timothy's yellow flower.

LEVEL 3 (APPLICATION)

* What would you have done if someone had given you a flower?

* Who in the neighborhood would help you take care of your flower. Why?

* Describe a type of flower box that Timothy could have made.

LEVEL 4 (ANALYSIS)

* Describe the relationship between Timothy and his grandmother.

* How was Mrs. Valdez different from other people who lived on Timothy's block?

* Describe Timothy's feelings about going to the park with his grandmother.

LEVEL 5 (SYNTHESIS)

* Name something else Timothy might have received during his visit to the park.

* What other ways could Timothy have taken care of his flower, besides using the ice cup?

* Imagine that Timothy wanted to grow flowers on his own. What would he need? How would he grow the flowers?

LEVEL 6 (EVALUATION)

* Predict what would have happened to the flower if Timothy had not heard the construction men outside of his house.

* Why was Mrs. Valdez always angry at the children on Timothy's block?

* What would the neighbors say if all the children on the block began to grow flowers? Would this change the neighborhood?

APPENDIX 1

Bloom's Taxonomy of Educational Objectives

KNOWLEDGE	SKILLS
1. Knowledge of specifics	define
	recognize
* knowledge of terminology	recall
* knowledge of specific facts	identify
	label
2. Knowledge of Ways and Means of Dealing With Specifics	understand
	examine
	show
* knowledge of conventions	collect
* knowledge of trends and sequences	
* knowledge of classifications and categories	
* knowledge of criteria	
* knowledge of methodology	
3. Knowledge of Universals and Abstractions in a Field	
* knowledge of principals and generalizations	
* knowledge of theories and structures	

COMPREHENSION

1. Translation	translate
	interpret
2. Interpretation	predict
	explain
3. Extrapolation	describe
	summarize

APPLICATION

	apply
1. Use Abstractions in Specific and Concrete Situations	solve
	experiment
	show

ANALYSIS

1. Analysis of Elements

2. Analysis of Relationships

3. Analysis of Organizational Principles

SYNTHESIS

1. Production of a Unique Communication

2. Production of a Plan for Operation

3. Derivation of a Set of Abstract Relations

EVALUATION

1. Judgments in Terms of Internal Evidence.

2. Judgments in Terms of External Evidence.

connect
relate
differentiate
classify
arrange
group
compare

design
redesign
combine
compose
construct
translate
imagine

interpret
judge
criticize
decide

APPENDIX ll

Verbs for Curriculum Development

Identification	Processes		
Model	Verb Delineation		
Taxonomy			
Knowledge	explain	relate	design
	show	code	interpret
Comprehension	list	take apart	judge
	observe	fill in	justify
Application	demonstrate	analyze	criticize
	uncover	take away	solve
Analysis	recognize	put together	decide
	discover	combine	
Synthesis	experiment	imagine	
	organize	suppose	
Evaluation	group	compare	
	collect	contrast	
	apply	add to	
	summarize	predict	
	order	assume	
	classify	translate	
	model	extend	
	construct	hypothesize	

Explanation: These verbs, randomly arranged beside the Taxonomy Model, are representative of the processes exemplified by the model.

APPENDIX III

What Happens to Students When Longer Wait-Times Occur?

1. The length of student responses increases. Explanatory statements increase from 400-800 percent.

2. The number of unsolicited but appropriate responses increases

3. Failure to respond decreases.

4. Confidence of children increases.

5. The incidence of speculative, creative thinking increases.

6. Teacher-centered teaching decreases, and student-centered interaction increases.

7. Students give more evidence before and after inference statements.

8. The number of questions asked by students increases.

9. The number of activities proposed by children increases.

10. Slow students contribute more: From 1.5 to 37 percent.

11. The variety of types of responses increases

12. Discipline problems decrease.

REFERENCES FOR CHILDREN'S LITERATURE
(LEVEL 1)

Bishop, Claire, H. & Wiese, Kurt. *The Five Chinese Brothers,* N.Y., Coward, McCann & Georghegan, 1938.

Brown, Marcia. *The Three Billy Goats Gruff,* N.Y., Scholastic Book Service, 1966.

Brown, Marcia & Perrault. *Cinderella,* N.Y., Scribner, 1954.

Craig, M. Jean. *The Three Wishes,* N.Y., Scribner, 1954.

deBrunoff, Jean. *The Story of Babar the Little Elephant,* N.Y., Random House, 1933.

de Paola, Tomie. *Helga's Dowry: A Troll Love Story,* N.Y., Harcourt, Brace & Jovanovich, 1977.

de Regnier, Beatrice S. *Little Red Riding Hood,* N.Y., Harcourt,Brace & Jovanovich, 1977.

Dyke, John. *Pigwig,* N.Y., Methuen, 1978.

Elkin, Benjamin. *Six Foolish Fishermen,* N.Y., Children's, 1957.

Farguhar, Margaret. *Goldilocks and the Three Bears,* N.Y., Grosset & Dunlap, 1958.

Galdone, Paul. *The Three Little Pigs,* N.Y., The Seabury Press, 1970.

Galdone, Paul. *Jack and the Beanstalk,* N.Y., The Seabury Press, 1968.

Galdone, Paul. *Henny Penny,* N.Y., The Seabury Press, 1968.

Garland, A. *Rumplestiltskin,* N.Y., Doubleday & Co., 1964.

Grimm, Brothers. *The Sleeping Beauty,* N.Y., Harcourt, Brace & Jovanovich, 1959.

Holl, Adelaide. *Sylvester, the Mouse with the Musical Ear,* N.Y., Western Pub. Co., 1961.

Hoban, Russell. *A Birthday for Frances,* N.Y., Harper & Row, 1968.

Jacobs, Joseph. *The Pied Piper,* N.Y., Cromwell Pub., 1978.

Leaf, Munro. *The Story of Ferdinand,* N.Y., Viking Press, 1936.

Lawrence, James. *Binky Brothers Detectives,* N.Y., Harper & Row, 1968.

McDermott, Gerald. *Arrow to the Sun,* N.Y., Holt, Rhinehart & Winston, 1973.

McDermott, Gerald. *The Magic Tree,* N.Y., Holt, Rhinehart & Winston, 1973.

Parish, Peggy. *Amelia Bedelia,* N.Y., Harper & Row, 1963.

Power, Barbara. *I Wish Laura's Mommy Was My Mommy,* N.Y., Lippincott, 1979.

Quigley, Lillian. *The Blind Men and the Elephant,* N.Y., Scribner, 1959.

Rey, H.A. *Curious George,* Boston, Houghton Mifflin, 1941.

Rockwell, Anne. *The Wolf Who Had a Wonderful Dream,* N.Y., Thomas Y. Crowell, 1973.

Steig, William. *Sylvester & the Magic Pebble,* N.Y., Simon and Schuster, 1969.

Udry, Janice M. *What Mary Jo Shared,* N.Y., Albert Whitman, 1966.

Viorst, Judith. *Alexander & the Terrible, Horrible, No Good, Very Bad Day,* N.Y., Atheneum, 1972.

Vanhalewiji, Mariette. *The Little Witch Wanda,* N.Y., World Pub. Co., 1970.

Zalbea, Jane B. *Will You Count the Stars Without Me?,* N.Y., Farrar Strauss, 1979.

REFERENCES FOR CHILDREN'S LITERATURE
(LEVEL 2)

Allard, Harry. *It's So Nice to Have a Wolf Around the House,* N.Y., Doubleday & Co., 1977.

Anderson, Lonzo & Adams, Adrienne. *Two Hundred Rabbits,* N.Y., The Viking Press, 1968.

Berg, Jean H. *There's Nothing To Do, So... Let Me Be You,* N.Y., West Minister Press, 1966.

Carrick, Carol. *The Accident,* N.Y., The Seabury Press, 1976.

Charnely, Nathaniel, & Charnley, Betty Jo. *Martha Ann & The Money Store,* New York, Harcourt, Brace and Jovanovich, 1973.

Christian, Mary B. *Nothing Much Happened Today,* N.Y., Addison-Wesley Pub., 1973.

Coombs, Patricia. *Lisa & The Grompet*, N.Y., Lothrop, Lee & Shepard Co., 1970.

Elkin, Benjamin. *The Loudest Noise In The World*, N.Y., The Viking Press, 1954.

Kellogg, Steven. *The Island of the Skog*, N. Y., The Dial Press, 1973.

Kent, Jack. *Dooly & The Snortsnoot*, N.Y., G. P. Putnam's & Sons, 1972.

Kraus, Robert, and Richter, Mischa. *Bunya The Witch*, N.Y., Windmill Books, 1971.

McGown, Tom. *Dragon Stew*, Il., Follett Pub, 1969.

Myers, Bernice. *The Apple War*, N.Y., Parents Magazine Press, 1973.

Peet, Bill. *Eli*, Mass., Houghton Mifflin Co., 1978.

Van Leeuwen, Jean. *Timothy's Flower*, N.Y., Random House, 1967.